"So, tell me what it's like to live on a ranch," she said. "Your kids must love it." Where had that come from? Little ripples of shock swept through B.J., followed by a crashing wave of mortification. If she could have crawled under the sofa, she would have. Immediately.

She looked at the slant of his shoulders and noticed there seemed to be a slight sag to them that wasn't there before. She wondered suddenly if his wife had died, and felt a sense of guilt for having brought up the subject. B.J. rose and moved to stand beside him. "I'm sorry," she said softly. "It's none of my business."

She heard the soft expletive that left his lips, no louder than a whisper on the wind, and knew that he was cursing his own defeat as much as she was chagrined by hers.

Her body trembled, and when his mouth touched the side of her neck, she moaned aloud and slipped her arms around his neck, dragging him closer.

"I thought one kiss would be enough," he said, his voice deep and rough, "but I was wrong."

His mouth was hard and hot on hers, hungry in its assault, demanding in its caress. She felt his need in that kiss, and an agony of loneliness that surprised her.

Raising his mouth from hers, he raised a hand to her face and, as his fingers traced the curve of her cheek, she found his touch almost unbearable in its tenderness. "I need you," he said softly, emotion deepening his voice. "I want to make love to you."

WHAT ARE *LOVESWEPT* ROMANCES?

They are stories of true romance and touching emotion. We believe those two very important ingredients are constants in our highly sensual and very believable stories in the LOVESWEPT line. Our goal is to give you, the reader, stories of consistently high quality that may sometimes make you laugh, sometimes make you cry, but are always fresh and creative and contain many delightful surprises within their pages.

Most romance fans read an enormous number of books. Those they truly love, they keep. Others may be traded with friends and soon forgotten. We hope that each LOVESWEPT romance will be a treasure—a "keeper." We will always try to publish

**LOVE STORIES YOU'LL NEVER FORGET
BY AUTHORS YOU'LL ALWAYS REMEMBER**

The Editors

TRICKS OF THE TRADE

CHERYLN BIGGS

BANTAM BOOKS
NEW YORK · TORONTO · LONDON · SYDNEY · AUCKLAND

TRICKS OF THE TRADE
A Bantam Book / May 1997

LOVESWEPT and the wave design are registered trademarks of Bantam Books, a division of Bantam Doubleday Dell Publishing Group, Inc. Registered in U.S. Patent and Trademark Office and elsewhere.

All rights reserved.
Copyright © 1997 by Cheryln Biggs.
Cover photo copyright © 1997 by Mort Engel Productions.
Floral border by Joyce Kitchell.
No part of this book may be reproduced or transmitted in any form or by any means, electronic or mechanical, including photocopying, recording, or by any information storage and retrieval system, without permission in writing from the publisher.
For information address: Bantam Books.

If you purchased this book without a cover you should be aware that this book is stolen property. It was reported as "unsold and destroyed" to the publisher and neither the author nor the publisher has received any payment for this "stripped book."

ISBN 0-553-44590-1

Published simultaneously in the United States and Canada

Bantam Books are published by Bantam Books, a division of Bantam Doubleday Dell Publishing Group, Inc. Its trademark, consisting of the words "Bantam Books" and the portrayal of a rooster, is Registered in U.S. Patent and Trademark Office and in other countries. Marca Registrada. Bantam Books, 1540 Broadway, New York, New York 10036.

PRINTED IN THE UNITED STATES OF AMERICA

OPM   10 9 8 7 6 5 4 3 2 1

This book is dedicated to Julie M, Sue, Jan, and Phyllis. Thanks for your support and words of encouragement.

And, of course, to Jack, my one and only hero.

ONE

"There's a Mr. Michael Gentry here who says it's urgent that he see you immediately in regard to the Charbonneau case."

B.J. looked up at her secretary and sighed. "Don't tell me the reward mongers are knocking at the door already."

The petite, gray-haired woman who acted more like B.J.'s mother than her secretary smiled. "I don't think so. At least not this one."

B.J. felt a start of surprise. "No? Then what?"

Alice Guilliox winked. "Well, why don't you just see him and find out."

"Fine, but give me a few minutes."

"Want me to take the pipsqueak out?" Alice asked, nodding toward the black and white mop of hair lying on the floor beside B.J.'s desk.

She smiled and looked down at the little dog that was half Pekingese, half poodle. She'd adopted the animal the year before when he'd been barely six months old. "No, he's alright, thanks."

As if knowing they were talking about him, he raised his head and yipped sharply.

"Beaujolais," B.J. admonished softly. "Quiet."

As Alice retreated from the office, closing the door as she went, Beaujolais went back to the business of taking a nap and B.J. turned in her chair and stared out the window. The day had started out extremely promising, which should have been a warning, because within no time it had spiraled straight downhill.

"Promising," she said with a scoff. "Right." Her grandmother had always said, when things seemed too good to be true, they probably were. But what else could she have considered a call from Mrs. Theodore Charbonneau? The woman was one of the wealthiest in New Orleans, and she'd called that morning to say she wanted to hire B.J. At the time B.J. had been thrilled, anticipating the influx of some desperately needed funds and long sought prestige for the agency. The fact that the wealthy socialite wasn't calling one of the city's more prominent investigative agencies should have given B.J. a clue that something wasn't quite right, but she'd been too excited to think about that.

Now she knew it was probably because none of the others would take the case. She drummed the fingers of her right hand on the wooden arm of her chair, in no hurry to see her first crackpot of the day. Alice had intimated that she didn't think this one was a crackpot, but B.J. was still suspicious. Alice wasn't always right. It could

Tricks of the Trade

be a wolf-in-sheep's-clothing kind of thing. After all, she'd been fooled before.

Normally the view of Jackson Square from her office in one of the Pontalba buildings was pleasant and tranquil, but today, with Mardi Gras in full swing, there were tourists and partygoers everywhere, almost all of them dressed in outrageously gaudy or ridiculous costumes. Of course the ancient walls and windows of the building, which bordered one side of the old square, could only do so much to mute the noise from outside.

Whirling around suddenly, the abrupt movement sending Beaujolais bolting up and skittering across the room, B.J. jabbed at the button on her intercom. She might as well see this guy and get it over with. "Show Mr. Gentry in, Alice, would you please?"

A moment later B.J.'s door opened. She rose, unconsciously brushing a lock of dark brown hair over her shoulder and giving a straightening tug to the red wool blazer she wore. Her gaze moved quickly over the man who walked toward her, his gait a lazy swagger that screamed arrogance, his golden Adonis good looks so devastating as to practically scorch her eyes. He seemed to exude cold, hard determination, while at the same time she sensed a nonchalance bordering on indolence that was unmistakable.

She studied his face feature by feature, searching for a flaw. When she saw the small line of a scar on his upper lip, she felt a little better. Her gaze swept over him again as he neared. *He's a man's man* and *a lady's man.* The thought flashed through her mind and filled her with apprehension, which agitated her.

Cheryln Biggs

4

She straightened her shoulders.

He was dressed in a sheepskin-lined denim jacket, faded jeans, a black Stetson that left a shadow hovering over his eyes, and a pair of badly scuffed cowboy boots. If he strapped a gun and holster around his hips, she was certain he'd look as if he had just walked through a time warp.

Beaujolais growled softly.

"Beau, that's enough," B.J. said. She forced a smile to her lips. "Mr. Gentry, good afternoon."

He ignored the dog as his gaze swept over B.J., coolly assessing.

Everything about him seemed rugged, from the set of his jaw to the hint of impudence in the slight curve of his lips. Physically he was probably as close as possible to being every woman's dream-come-true, including hers, a fact which did nothing to improve her mood. She guessed him at around six feet tall, with classical features that had a rough-hewn edge to them, as if carved with a pick and hammer rather than a sculptor's knife. His body appeared lean and muscular, and beneath thick golden brows were a pair of penetrating blue eyes that looked *as if they might be able to see right into a person's soul.* B.J. shook the ridiculous thought away. After her last disastrous romantic liaison she'd sworn off men, at least for awhile, so whatever Mr. Michael Gentry was or wasn't didn't matter.

"I'm B.J. Poydras," she said, and offered her hand. The look that had momentarily flashed onto his face as he'd stepped into her office had more than told her he hadn't known beforehand that private investigator B.J. Poydras was a woman.

Tricks of the Trade

But then most people didn't, unless they'd been referred by a previous client.

"Thanks for seeing me on such short notice." His voice was deep, as if rising from the depths of the earth, his accent a seeming blend of big city rush and high country drawl.

His long, thick fingers, strong and full of power, wrapped around her slender ones like an enveloping blanket. B.J. immediately assessed his handshake. It was firm yet gentle, which surprised her. The handshakes of most men were usually one or the other, rarely both.

He met her gaze square on and B.J. found that his eyes reminded her of a cloudless summer sky, filled with promises of laughter and joy. Yet at the same time, the shadowy black pupils situated in the center of those infinite pools of blue seemed to hint at something dark and ominous that the onlooker just might be better off avoiding.

B.J. found herself unable to look away. She tried to appear unruffled and professional as she pulled her hand from his.

Smiling, and finally able to break the almost hypnotic hold he had on her, she motioned him to one of the two burgundy leather chairs that faced her desk. "Please, Mr. Gentry, have a seat."

As he moved to sit down, one side of his jacket fell slightly away from his body, and B.J. caught a flash of silver at his waist.

She settled into her own chair and tried to regather her composure, but after that brief glimpse at what was hidden under his jacket, she was finding composure a difficult thing to gather. "You told my secretary that it was imperative you speak with me about the Charbonneau case. Do you have information on it?"

She looked directly into his eyes, waiting for him to answer. If he was a cop, which that flash of silver gave her every reason to believe he was, he would want information from her, but he wouldn't give any. That was the way it always worked. She realized too late that she shouldn't have looked straight into his eyes. His gaze had captured hers again and seemed intent on holding it prisoner, those blue depths that had reminded her of a summer sky, peaceful and lazy, revealing no hint of mercy or inclination to allow her escape.

A second later B.J. nearly sagged in relief when he looked away, reaching up to remove his hat, setting it on a corner of her desk, then glancing down and pulling a wallet from the inside pocket of his jacket. Curls of dark blond, almost golden hair caught the sunlight that poured in through the windows to the right of B.J.'s desk.

The short, silent encounter would have merely been called good eye contact by some, but B.J. was now categorizing it as more like a tug of wills. It left her frustrated with herself and angry at him.

"I need your cooperation, Miss Poydras." He flipped the well-worn wallet open and held it out to her at the same time that he pulled back his jacket to reveal the badge she'd already glimpsed. The identification card in the wallet not only verified his name, but also the words emblazoned across the badge: *U.S. Marshal.*

B.J.'s brows rose, momentarily masking her annoyance. She sat back and crossed her arms.

Tricks of the Trade

7

"A cop," she said, "what a sincere pleasure." The words were cordial enough, but her tone was laced with a sarcasm she didn't even bother to try to hide.

He seemed to ignore the edge of contempt in her voice and shoved the wallet back into his pocket, then propped one foot onto his other knee. "U.S. Marshal," he corrected, his deep tone holding just a hint of rancor.

B.J. did a purposely slow flutter of her long, dark lashes and forced a smile to her lips. "And just what is it that brings a *U.S. Marshal* to my doorstep?"

"I want you to tell me everything you know about Theodore Charbonneau."

Surprise left her momentarily silent.

"I also want to know why Charbonneau's wife hired you. Was it to prove him dead or find him alive? And I need to know everything and anything you uncover while working this case."

B.J.'s mouth had dropped slightly open as he'd talked. Now, one gracefully arched brow soared upward, an unconscious habit when she was annoyed—and at the moment that description was a gross understatement. "First of all, Marshal . . ."

"Call me Mick."

B.J. fumed. There were other things she'd rather call him, but she was trying to remain polite and professional.

Too bad he's a cop.

The thought was there, unbidden, unwanted, and unwelcome, before she had a chance to throw a roadblock up against it. She stiffened. Cop, cowboy, or alien creature from another planet, it didn't matter because she didn't care.

"As I was saying, Marshal," B.J. said, her tone haughty and laced with frost, "whoever hires me and whatever happens while I'm on their case is privileged information."

"Not this time."

She wanted to bolt from her chair and order him to leave her office. Give him a karate chop to the midriff and watch him double over. So instead she used every ounce of self-discipline she had to remain seated and at least appear calm. "Get my client to cooperate with you, Marshal, and I will too."

"I've already talked to your client, Miss Poydras. She clammed up, except to refer me to you."

B.J. shrugged, feeling a spurt of satisfaction. It wasn't often she had something the authorities wanted. "Sorry."

His foot slammed to the floor, and the harsh thud of his boot against the old, scarred hardwood caused B.J. to start.

Beaujolais darted across the room, crouched in front of Mick, and growled, ready to attack his boot if he moved even a hair.

"Beau, no," B.J. said sharply.

The little dog stopped growling and lay down, but he didn't take his eyes off of Mick's boot.

Mick leaned forward, scowling. "Look, Miss Poydras, I frankly don't give a damn about confidence and privileged information. I'm after an escaped con who's somehow involved with Charbonneau, maybe even killed him, which means I need your full cooperation on this thing."

"Killed him?"

"Yes, as in murder. The way I understand it, NOPD

has a body in the morgue that's supposedly your client's husband, and I'm not totally convinced his condition wasn't intentional."

B.J.'s thoughts spun. She hadn't been hired to investigate a murder, and as far as she knew the police hadn't ruled Charbonneau's death a homicide. She shook her head. "I'm sorry, Marshal, but you're mistaken. Mr. Charbonneau died when his cabin caught on fire. It was an accident."

One corner of Mick's mouth quirked upward slightly. "Are you sure?"

"The police seem satisfied."

"If they were satisfied, Miss Poydras, the case would be closed . . ."—he stared at her long and hard, as if to emphasize his next words—". . . and it's not."

B.J.'s chin rose to a defiant slant. "That's only because positive identification of the body hasn't been made yet."

Mick rose, walked to the window, and looked out at the square.

B.J. watched him, feeling exceedingly and unexplainably wary now.

He turned. "I hear that since the guy was burned beyond recognition and his false teeth are missing, a positive ID isn't likely."

B.J. remained silent as he returned to his seat.

"Which makes me wonder just why Mrs. Charbonneau hired you."

"Sorry," B.J. said, "that's privileged information."

Their glaring gazes locked, each challenging the other and refusing to back down.

Cheryln Biggs

10

Mick tried to keep his irritation hidden but he knew it was probably blazing from his face like a neon sign. He just didn't know whether he was more annoyed at her lack of cooperation or the fact that from the moment he'd walked into her office and realized B.J. Poydras was a woman, his overactive imagination, prodded into overtime by a suddenly simmering libido, had been conjuring up images it had absolutely no business conjuring up.

He smiled, exerting a show of patience he normally didn't have. She was too beautiful, too sensual, and too damned tempting. A string of curses pranced through Mick's mind as he stared at her, the coldness emanating from his eyes masking the heat building within his body.

Her eyes were the color of the desert sky at dusk, a deep, warm blue touched by sparks of gold, while her nose was turned up just enough at the end to give her a look of defiant sassiness. And her lips . . . if they weren't made for kissing he'd eat his damned hat.

Another parade of curses danced through his mind. This meeting was not going at all the way he'd planned. He'd figured to come in, flash his badge, explain himself, get the cooperation and the information he needed, and that would be that. Instead, his mind was split down the middle like George Washington's cherry tree, half concentrating on the business of getting her to cooperate in his quest to catch Carl Townsend, the other half filled with images of her in his bed, naked, hot, and passionate.

Exerting more willpower than he'd known he had, Mick closed down the traitorous thoughts, shoving them to the back of his mind and slamming a door on them. All he wanted from her was professional cooperation. No personal relationship, not even a short one. No one-night stands or temporary flings. He'd tried those in the past and they didn't work. And he'd tried the longer kind, too, the commitment kind: marriage, home, and a kid, and he'd blown it, big time. That was a mistake he didn't plan on making again.

"Miss Poydras, maybe if I explain the reason I need this information it will clear up a few things for you and you'll understand why I must have your cooperation."

B.J. bristled at his condescending tone, and the request itself. How many times had she asked the cops for help and been turned down? "It won't matter, Marshal. I'm not about to break my client's confidence."

Mick sat forward, the fire of anger darkening his eyes. "You'd rather protect an ex-con, possibly a murderer? Let him get away, maybe to kill again?"

Her own temper flared. "You don't know that someone has been murdered."

"And you don't know that someone hasn't been," he snapped back. "So at least listen to what I have to say."

Beaujolais, obviously not liking Mick's tone, crouched menacingly, rear raised, hackles up, and growled.

"Beau, come here," B.J. said, her tone stern.

The little dog ran around the desk and jumped into B.J.'s lap. With one hand on the animal's back, she stared up at Mick, her jaw set tight, eyes fiery with anger.

Mick took her silence for acquiescence. "Five years ago Carl Townsend and a couple of his buddies robbed a bank and got away. He was eventually caught and sent to prison and his buddies were killed, but the money from the robbery was never recovered."

"I don't see where this has anything to do with Theodore or Lillian Charbonneau," B.J. said.

"Carl escaped about six weeks ago. Three weeks later he turned up in San Francisco and purchased a ring with a credit card in the name of Theodore Charbonneau."

"That's impossible."

"That's fact," Mick retorted. "And it's also the name of your client's supposedly dead husband."

"That doesn't mean anything. Lillian's company has an office in San Francisco, and her husband oversaw its operations. Anyway, how do you know Theodore wasn't the one who bought the ring and used his charge card?"

"You're investigating the man's alleged death. Was he in San Francisco three weeks ago?"

B.J. felt like throttling him. Answering a question with a question was an old trick, and always effective. She wanted to stare at him and say, "I don't know, was he?" But that would sound stupid, and anyway, she knew the answer to that question, or she would in a second. She jerked open the file Alice had just made for the Charbonneau case and looked at the itinerary Lillian Charbonneau had provided her for Theodore's activities for the two months prior to his death. B.J. looked back up at Mick and smiled, knowing full well, smugness was emanating from her face like a blinding light. "Yes," she said simply, "he was."

"More proof it was my guy who used the charge card with Charbonneau's approval."

"What?" B.J. stared in astonishment.

Tricks of the Trade

Mick smiled. "Charbonneau was there at the time it was used, he wasn't the one who used it, and he didn't report it missing or stolen. I lost Townsend's trail for a few days after he escaped—"

"That was probably a first," B.J. said with a sneer.

"As a matter of fact, it was," Mick said. "Anyway, I was pretty sure by the route he was taking that he was heading for San Francisco, and I contacted one of our informants there."

"How convenient."

The blaze of controlled annoyance that swept through his eyes made her feel like cringing in self-defense, but she fought against the reaction.

"To make a long story short, Miss Poydras, when I got to the hotel my informant said Townsend was supposed to be staying in, we checked the description of all the patrons and came up with only one possibility, the guy who'd checked out that morning. John Smithson. I had a team come in, dust the room for prints, and Smithson turned out to be Townsend. The charge slip for the ring was in the trash can, and our experts say the signature on it was forged by Townsend."

Mick sat back, folded his arms across his chest, and stared at her. "Okay, I told you my story, and it should be pretty obvious why I need your cooperation."

B.J. opened her mouth to respond, then abruptly closed it. He might know that Mrs. Charbonneau had hired her, but she wasn't about to tell him that it was to find the woman's missing prize-winning poodle, not determine whether Theodore Charbonneau was dead or not. Lillian Charbonneau didn't give two figs about her husband, though B.J. was pretty certain the widow wouldn't want that little tidbit of information bandied about.

"I figure there's several possibilities," Mick continued. "Townsend could have mugged Charbonneau and stolen his credit cards, but I've checked and they weren't reported stolen. I thought for awhile that maybe Townsend and Charbonneau were the same person, but after I checked I knew that was out."

"So?" B.J. said.

"So I figure they're not one and the same man, but they are connected somehow. Maybe through some kind of shady dealings, maybe through a mutual friend, or maybe their meeting was just a fluke. Charbonneau could have been mugged by Townsend or some street punk who then sold the charge card to Townsend. Whatever, if it was a mugging, Charbonneau had some kind of reason not to admit or report it. Maybe he was seeing another woman, had her with him when it happened and figured if he reported it and his wife got wind of the thing, that would be that. Divorce time. I don't know."

B.J. shook her head. "No. It's impossible, really. Theodore Charbonneau was an upstanding citizen."

"Yeah? Well now he's most likely a dead one," Mick said, "or he's in cahoots with Carl Townsend and it's some other poor slob lying in the morgue burnt to a crisp. Maybe it's even Carl himself." Mick sat forward, anger and frustration hardening his features further, the coldness in his eyes sniping at her. "Whatever's going on here, it's pretty clear my case has taken a nosedive into yours and—" He abruptly paused, struggling to rein in his temper. He'd been about to demand her cooperation again, but if there was one thing he'd learned all too well since becoming a marshal, it was how to read people, and the set of her jaw told him that demanding her cooperation wasn't going to work now any more than it had a few minutes ago.

He changed course. "And I think we should work together on this thing."

"Work together?" B.J. sputtered. She'd almost risen out of her chair, and the movement had thrown Beaujolais to the floor. The dog landed with a thud, righted himself with a haughty glance at B.J., and curled up a few feet away. "But I'm not—" She nearly bit off the end of her tongue in order to stop herself from telling him that he was totally mistaken, that her case didn't involve finding out whether Theodore Charbonneau was dead, alive, or had run off with another woman—or an ex-con. What it did involve was playing pet detective and finding Mrs. C.'s precious dog, ChiChi. And that was all.

"Look," Mick said, breaking into her thoughts, "working together makes good sense. With your knowledge of the territory here, and my official contacts, we could save a lot of time and grief by not tripping over each other and covering the same ground twice, and we could probably have this case solved in no time."

Work together. The words echoed through her mind. B.J.'s fingers drummed lightly on her desk as her thoughts spun. She'd been hired to find Mrs. C.'s dog, which had disappeared the same time as Mrs. C.'s husband, but unlike Theodore—if that's whose body was in the morgue—the dog hadn't been found at the cabin, dead or alive. B.J. frowned. Theodore's car hadn't been at the cabin either, and she knew that the police were also speculating that maybe the fire wasn't an accident, that maybe Theodore had committed suicide and had driven the car into the bayou first. Which meant ChiChi had probably become gator bait. But what if that wasn't what had happened?

B.J. raised her eyes to find Mick Gentry watching her. "Well?" he said, catching her gaze.

"I'm thinking." She looked away again. What if what he suggested was right? What if Theodore Charbonneau had been murdered, or had left someone else's body at the cabin in his place and was still alive? That would mean he still had ChiChi, whom she had been hired to find, so shouldn't she follow up that lead?

B.J. almost groaned aloud. She didn't want to work with a U.S. marshal. More to the point, she didn't want to work with *this* U.S. marshal. She looked back at him and made a quick decision—one she knew he wasn't going to like. She would follow up the theory on her own. "Look, Marshal, I'll keep you informed if I find out anything I think you should know, okay?" She reached for a pen and paper. "What hotel are you staying at?"

"Not good enough," Mick answered.

B.J. shot him a withering glower as her fingers squeezed the pen. Why did the handsome ones always have to make life so damned difficult? Or maybe all men were like that. She wasn't sure. She'd never dated an ugly man, but she was beginning to think it was about time she started. Maybe she'd start with that nice guy at the bank who always waited on her. He had a nose like a water-

Tricks of the Trade

logged cantaloupe and wore glasses that looked like the bottom of soda pop bottles, but so what? Mort Kluzzicker was probably the nicest guy on the face of the earth.

And I'm not attracted to him in the least.

She forced her attention back to the business at hand, which was getting Mr. U.S. Marshal Michael Gentry out of her office. "Look, sharing information is the best I can offer. I usually work alone."

"Yeah, so do I. Less complicated that way, but this time I think we should make an exception."

"No."

Mick was suddenly torn between two desires. One prodded him to lunge across her desk, wrap his fingers around that long beautiful column of neck, and strangle her. The other urged him to reach across her desk, drag her to him, and capture those "made for kissing" lips with his. Neither was a viable option, neither was feasible, and that he could even think of the latter one only infuriated him. He rose. "Look, maybe you don't understand the situation here, Miss Poydras. I've got an ex-con who's connected in some way with your—"

"I understand the situation perfectly, Marshal Gentry," B.J. retorted, getting angrier by the minute at his patronizing tone and manner, and more uncomfortable by her growing awareness of his masculinity, "but we are not working together."

The scowl that suddenly twisted his face was so dark, it seemed to take over the room. "Fine," he said with a growl, grabbing his hat and standing, "then consider me a shadow, lady. One that you're not going to be able to shake until I get what I want."

TWO

B.J. stared at the big brown bear dancing on the walkway that separated her office building from Jackson Square. He did a cartwheel, jumped onto the black wrought iron fence that surrounded the square, and shook his derriere, and the blue ribbon attached to it, at a passerby. Then he noticed B.J. watching, raised the baby rattle he was holding, and waved it at her. She smiled and returned the wave. It wasn't the most original Mardi Gras costume she'd ever seen, but whoever was inside the thing was definitely making the most of it, and keeping warm in the chill March air. She moved back to her desk and flopped down in her chair.

The Charbonneau case folder lay open before her, but there wasn't much to see. Other than Theodore's itinerary for the past two months, and the phone numbers of every dog shelter, humane society, city pound, and animal adoption agency Alice could find, she had nothing.

Nothing, that is, except a U.S. marshal who had

threatened to hound her every step. And the possibility now that Theodore Charbonneau had been involved in something his wife would definitely not approve of. And the further possibility that the man might even still be alive, which B.J. had a feeling Lillian Charbonneau wouldn't approve of either.

She nearly groaned aloud and began to wind a lock of hair around her finger. She scanned the sparse information again, trying to determine what her next step should be, and decided she should have kept watching the dancing bear. At least he'd made her smile. This case was already about to cause her to scream, and she hadn't even been on it for a full day.

But if she was truthful with herself, which she usually was, it wasn't the case that had her upset, it was the U.S. marshal who had attached himself to it.

"I take it you told him you wouldn't work with him."

B.J. looked up to see Alice standing in the doorway, hands on hips, motherly frown on her face.

"You take right," she said. "I don't see any reason for it."

"No reason? Hah! How about the fact that he's just about the most devastatingly handsome thing ever to cross this threshold. Maybe to enter this entire city," she smiled slyly, "since Clint Eastwood did his movie here, that is. The Marshal might be too young for me—Lord knows if I brought someone that young home my sons would think I'd gone crazy and have me committed—but he's just right for you, and you're going to let him slip right through your fingers."

"I've been engaged three times in the past five years,"

B.J. said, releasing the lock of hair she'd been playing with, picking up a pencil and twirling it between her fingers, "so stop playing matchmaker, Alice, it's useless."

"You're just hard to please."

B.J. laughed. "They're the ones who broke the engagements, remember?"

Alice smiled. Though she looked like the fairy godmother in Cinderella, B.J. knew that when Alice was scheming to find her a man, she was anything but innocent.

"Don't even think about it, Alice, really. I don't like him."

Mick watched a big brown bear prance across the walkway, shake a baby rattle and his beribboned rear end at the tourists who'd paused to watch him, and silently flirt with several older women who laughed raucously at his antics. What no one but Mick seemed to notice was that while the bear drew everyone's attention, a petite young woman dressed as a gypsy, in cascading veils and strings of golden beads, was moving quietly through the crowd and picking every pocket she could.

Mick tried to decide what to do. If he made a move to arrest her, the bear would take off. If he went for the bear, he'd lose the girl. And it wasn't his problem anyway. He took a small cellular phone from the pocket of his jacket, flipped it open, and called the local police emergency number.

Odds were, by the time the cops arrived, the girl and the bear would be gone, along with a lot of tourists' wal-

Tricks of the Trade

lets. Nevertheless, he was a cop, and he couldn't just ignore that a crime was occurring.

After talking to NOPD dispatch, Mick returned the phone to his pocket, looked around, then glanced at his watch. For a split second the sight of the silver and turquoise band reminded him of the time he had taken Kyle and Sherry to New Mexico on vacation. Sherry had bought him the watch as an anniversary present. He pushed the memory away. That had been a long time ago, another lifetime, and another Mick Gentry.

He sighed deeply. It was almost four-thirty. Too early to go back to his hotel, too early to eat dinner. Anyway, he'd told B.J. Poydras that he was going to be her shadow, and if that's what it was going to take to get her to cooperate with him, then that's what he was going to do.

A slight breeze from the nearby river swept past and brushed the back of his neck, stirring the ragged curls that lay there and sending a chill snaking down Mick's back. He shivered and yanked up the fleece-lined collar of his jacket. Then, stepping into a shadowed alcove, he leaned back against the brick building, drawing his left leg up and pressing his booted heel against the wall.

Within seconds a cop on horseback appeared, riding around the corner of the church at one end of the square and toward the crowd still watching the dancing bear. Another police officer approached on foot from the opposite, river side of the square. The mounted one zeroed in on the bear, the other one on the girl.

Mick was impressed. He'd figured that with how crowded the Quarter's streets were with Mardi Gras celebrants, not to mention the obvious troublemakers and drunks, the local cops wouldn't show up for awhile.

Within minutes both the bear and gypsy were in handcuffs.

The sun was just dropping below the roofline of the building on the opposite side of the square, an exact duplicate of the one Mick was standing in front of, when B.J. Poydras left her office.

But she surprised him. Instead of heading for a car, she walked across the wide thoroughfare that separated the French Quarter from the docks and onto one of the riverboats.

Mick cursed. "Now what in the hell is she doing?"

Hurrying to the small ticket booth that stood beside the boat's ramp, Mick bent to talk to the older woman sitting inside. He pointed toward the riverboat. "Is that boat going somewhere?"

She looked as if he'd just asked her if the world was still spinning. "Well, of course it is, honey."

Mick forced himself to remain calm and not snap out his next question. He didn't like uninformative answers, and he didn't like to be called "honey" by strangers. "Where?"

"On a cruise, of course." She smiled. "Would you like a ticket, honey? It includes dinner."

Mick glanced at the boat. The last time he'd gotten on a boat he'd gotten seasick. He'd turned green and thought he was going to die. Of course that had been ten years ago, and he'd been on a charter fishing boat out of San Francisco, and the sea had been so choppy he could have sworn someone had taken an eggbeater to it.

Tricks of the Trade

23

It was not a pleasant memory.

"Honey? The *Natchez* is going to leave in ten minutes, if you want to get on."

As if to emphasize her words, a whistle on the boat blew.

Mick looked at the woman again. He could get on the boat and watch B.J., or he could wait on the dock for her to return. But what if she was meeting someone on board? Maybe someone connected to the case somehow? Maybe she was following up a lead. He couldn't chance it. "Give me a ticket," he muttered, and felt his stomach turn over.

A minute later he walked up the ramp and said a silent prayer that the Mississippi wouldn't prove as choppy as the waters beyond the Golden Gate Bridge had. He found B.J. in the lounge, talking to a man who, judging from his outfit, Mick assumed was a maitre d'.

Mick swept the Stetson from his head and stepped out of the doorway and behind a gathering of people so that B.J. wouldn't see him.

The sound of a calliope suddenly filled the air, accompanied by the screaming burst of a steam whistle. The huge paddle wheel at the rear of the boat began to churn the water and the vessel moved away from the dock.

Mick felt his stomach begin to roll and tried to ignore his sudden queasiness by focusing on B.J. and attempting to read her lips as she talked. It didn't work, and he was too far away from her, to be able to overhear her, so if the maitre d' had something to do with the Charbonneau case, Mick was out of luck.

On the other hand, she could have been doing nothing more than discussing what was on the menu for dinner, or where she wanted to sit.

Mick's stomach roiled and he clenched his teeth.

Minutes later, as the boat moved farther and farther toward the middle of the river, Mick followed B.J. from the lounge into the gift shop, where she talked for several minutes with the sales clerk. Then she moved back through the lounge and into the room beyond.

The smell of roast beef, baked potatoes, and a variety of other foods hit Mick the moment he walked into the room. He saw B.J. pick up a plate and begin to ladle food onto it. His stomach did a cartwheel, and he did an abrupt U-turn. He could almost feel his cheeks turning green and the sandwich he'd had for lunch looking for an escape route.

Cursing himself and his weakness, he strode across the deck, tossing his hat onto a nearby chair as he made a beeline for the railing. He grasped it tightly, stared out into the twilight, and tried to ignore the gentle sway of the boat as it rode across the lapping, murky waves. Mick breathed deeply, hoping the cold evening air would calm his insides and relax his body.

Half an hour later, finally feeling as if he could move away from the railing without disaster striking, Mick turned to reenter the room where he'd last seen B.J. A soda would help settle his stomach. He stopped when he saw her standing only a few yards away, beside the huge red paddle wheel that was pushing the boat down the river.

He watched her walk toward him, her dark hair gently blowing about her shoulders, her hips swaying seductively, blue eyes steadily holding his as if she knew exactly what effect she was having on his body, on his thoughts, and was daring him to put them into action.

His gaze dropped to her mouth as she neared, skimming over the perfectly defined upper lip, then over the slightly fuller bottom one that, just for a split second, he thought he saw tremble slightly. Desire snapped through him like a bolt of lightning, hot and fierce. Mick suddenly wanted nothing more than to reach out and drag her into his arms, crush her body to his, feel the warmth of her flesh, and taste the sweetness of those lips that he felt certain had been made just to torture him.

"I didn't find out anything on your case," she said, pausing before him, one dark brow rising slightly as she spoke.

Her words abruptly jerked Mick from his fantasies.

"So you followed me, Marshal." She smiled smugly. "And got yourself seasick for nothing."

He felt his green cheeks turn red and hoped the dim lights on the deck didn't illuminate him enough so that she could see he was actually blushing like a teenager. "It was just something I ate this morning, Miss Poydras. Been bothering me all day."

Choking back a chuckle, B.J. said, "Right. Probably all that rich Southern food you're not used to." She turned to walk away, then paused and looked back at him. "Oh, and for your information, Marshal, I called the coroner after you left my office this afternoon. They haven't finished with the tests, but they're still assuming that the body in the morgue is Theodore Charbonneau, and that he died in and because of the fire, which is still labeled an accident."

"The key word," Mick said, as she started to walk away from him again, "is 'assuming.'"

B.J. looked back at him and asked herself for what was probably the thousandth time since she'd begun to notice boys as a teenager, why the handsome ones always also had to be the most troublesome ones. Any other time she'd probably be drooling over him, every cell in her body aching to know what it would feel like to be held by him, kissed by him, not to mention made love to by him.

It took only a millisecond for her gaze to rake over him and reconfirm that everything Alice had said was true. Part rugged cowboy, part James Bond, and probably the best looking specimen of human male that had ever walked on Louisiana soil, he was also proving to be a real pain. B.J. didn't like being questioned. She didn't like being followed, didn't like anyone poking his nose into her case, and she definitely didn't like a man whose gaze made her feel as if he were peeling off her clothes with his eyes—which is exactly what she felt like every time she looked at Marshal Mick Gentry.

She smiled. "Like I said earlier, Marshal, you work your case and I'll work mine." Which is exactly what she had been doing on the riverboat, though she wasn't about to share that information with him. The maitre d' and his wife, the gift shop saleslady, also bred poodles, and had been the ones who had sold ChiChi to Mrs. Charbonneau. B.J. had hoped they would put out the word in their circles that the dog was missing, and also give her a lead on where else she could search for him. They'd both said they would be more than happy to alert everyone they dealt with that ChiChi was missing, but had no idea where the dog might be, unless it had been sold on the black market—a definite possibility, since ChiChi had won top prizes at several of the biggest dog shows in the last year. Or, they suggested, ChiChi could merely be lost in the bayou, only to become a gator's hors d'oeuvre.

B.J. had already thought of that one and prayed it wasn't true.

Tipping her head toward Mick in a final gesture of dismissal, B.J. disappeared into the throng of people milling about the lounge.

He thought about going after her, felt his stomach object at even the thought of movement, and turned back to the railing. He didn't know what it was about B.J. Poydras that made her get under his skin, but she definitely did, and he didn't like it. There was no room in his life for those kinds of complications. And even if there was, he didn't want them. He clutched the railing, stared into the night, ignored everything else, and ordered his stomach to calm down.

As he breathed deeply of the river's unique musky scent, he remembered another trip he'd taken, long ago, where the night had been full of stars and the water had held its own scent and magic. His mind spun back in time, old memories that he usually kept locked away racing forth to invade his thoughts before he had a chance to stop them.

It had been just after he'd wrapped up a rather gruesome case. He hadn't been with the service that long and felt in the need of a vacation, a breather, something to make him forget the horrors of what he'd been a part of. A friend had suggested he take a few days off and recommended a small resort on the beach of Carmel. That's when he'd met Sherry. She had been working at one of the local stores. Within six months they were married. Six months after that Kyle had been born. Everything had gone fine for awhile, then Kyle had started school and Sherry had started complaining. Mick was gone too much, he spent more time on the job than at home, and even when he was home he seemed to still be on the job, always working at his desk or talking to another officer or a contact on the phone.

Mick sighed and pushed the thoughts from his mind. He didn't want to think about the day that it had all ended, that day four years earlier when his world had been so savagely torn apart. It had nearly destroyed him, and sometimes, especially at night when he was alone with his thoughts and memories, he still wished it had.

"Rotten husband and father material." Those had been Sherry's parting words, thrown at him the day she'd finally left him, and he couldn't disagree. Not then, and not now. Maybe if he had tried harder before that day, things would have been different.

A long sigh slipped from his lips, and he reached up to brush a lock of hair from his forehead, whipped there by the wind. The haunting, lonely ache that had been born the day Kyle had been ripped away from them was still with Mick, and he knew it always would be, a dark, gnawing hole in his heart. For months afterward he'd refused to work or go out. He'd cried a million tears and cursed everyone and everything. Then, with the help of his

Tricks of the Trade

friends, he finally managed to pull himself together. The ache of loss was at least bearable now, as long as he kept working and didn't think about it too much.

As long as he didn't think about how much he'd loved and lost, about the son he would never see again.

The boat whistle snagged his attention. Mick wiped a tear from his eye, turned, and saw that the *Natchez* was heading back toward the wharf.

People began moving out onto the deck, preparing to disembark. Mick squared his shoulders, forcing his memories into the dark recesses of his mind where they belonged while he was on a case. He pulled on the cold cloak of his job, his protection against the world, against himself, then looked around for B.J. Finally spotting her, he grabbed his hat and tried to weave his way through the crowd toward her.

She was down the ramp, across the wharf, and halfway across Decatur Street by the time he made his way off the boat. He reached the curb just in time to see her drive by. Smiling, she waved to him, and a second later her snazzy little black sports car disappeared around a corner.

After a near sleepless night filled with one haunting dream after another, Mick rose, shuffled into the bathroom, and, splashing his face with cold water, looked in the mirror. The image that stared back at him wasn't, in his opinion, a very pretty sight. In fact, it was pretty gruesome. Harsh. Haggard. "Maybe I should change my name to Godzilla," he said to his image.

An hour later, after doing a quick five-mile jog

through the Quarter's still-empty streets, then returning to the hotel to stand in the shower and let a deluge of water pour over his body, Mick felt a little more like a real, live person. Or as close to one as he figured he was ever going to get again.

He grabbed his jacket from the chair he'd thrown it onto the night before, slipped it on, and left the hotel. "First line of business," he mumbled as he unlocked the door of his rental car, a nondescript sedan, "is another visit to the city's ghoul."

Ten minutes later he walked into the hallway leading to the coroner's office, rounded a corner, and ran smack into B.J. Poydras on her way out. Her breasts pushed into his chest, the top of her head skimmed underneath his chin, she stepped on his foot, and one of her legs . . . he decided not to think about what her leg had done, concentrating instead on remaining upright, gritting his teeth, holding on to her arms, and forcing a smile to his lips until the pain shooting through his loins subsided.

B.J. looked up at him, stunned to realize that the wall she thought she'd run into was Mick Gentry. The moment the thought entered her mind it was immediately overrun by another, a curse that he'd seen her.

She wasn't about to admit to him or anyone else that she needed money so badly, she had agreed to play pet detective for Mrs. C. She also didn't want to reinforce his suggestion that since they were both more or less on the same case, they should work together. And she feared that was exactly what he was going to say again . . . if she gave him the chance.

Her thoughts raced, but instead of trying to twist

Tricks of the Trade

31

away from him, she inexplicably remained still. She'd been on her way to check out a "found" ad in the animal column of the local paper when she'd decided, since it was on the way, to stop at the morgue and see if they'd verified that it was Theodore Charbonneau lying there, and not someone else. If it was someone else, then no doubt Theo had taken off for parts unknown and ChiChi was with him. In that case she could forget checking out her lead and probably say good-bye to the bonus Mrs. C. had hung before her like a carrot in front of a rabbit.

Unfortunately, the lab reports weren't final and the verdict was still up in the air.

She finally got her senses back and tried to back away from him, but found herself locked in a grip as secure as a steel vice. B.J. stiffened. "If you're okay now," she said, her tone icy, "you can let go of me."

Mick looked down and smiled, forgetting that just a few hours earlier he'd sworn to do nothing but eat, drink, and breathe business until this case was done and he had Carl Townsend in custody. And that included sticking to business when he was around B.J. Poydras. Now, with her body only a hairbreath from his, his fingers were burning as if on fire while he held on to her arms, and the tantalizing scent of her perfume . . . like jasmine on the night air . . . was causing his mind to go off on a bent of imaginative seduction.

Danger bells went off in his head at her words, and he jerked his hands away from her at the same moment B.J. tried to pull back. She lost her balance, and Mick grabbed her again to keep her from falling backward.

"Don't do that," she snapped, trying to twist away from him.

He released her again, swallowed the curt retort he'd been about to mutter, and smiled instead. "Sorry, I guess next time you'd rather I let you bounce off the floor."

"I wasn't going to fall," B.J. said, knowing full well, that's exactly what she would have done if he hadn't caught her again. But he didn't have to know that. "And there won't be a next time."

"Good. So what'd you learn in there?" He nodded toward the door to the coroner's office, then leaned one shoulder lazily against the wall as he stared down at her.

"Nothing." She took a step back, fussed at the sapphire-colored blazer that had become slightly mussed at their collision, and worked at not looking at him. The man exuded more masculinity than a roomful of male strippers, and whether she liked it or not, her heart was pounding like an Indian war drum and her pulse was racing as if her veins were the Indy 500 track. She was obviously not immune. "I mean," she said, wanting nothing more now than to get away from him, "the coroner didn't have anything new to say. They still assume it's Charbonneau's body and the fire was an accident."

Mick's smile widened. "Assume."

B.J. bristled and brushed past him. "Excuse me, Marshal, but I have some things to do."

He'd promised himself he was going to be nice to her. He was going to charm her into cooperating. He was going to be the epitome of niceness even if it killed him, which it just might do if she didn't thaw out a bit pretty soon. Because in spite of the fact that his libido was going

Tricks of the Trade

crazy and his blood was turning to fire at just watching her walk, he still wanted to strangle her for being so obstinate. "So, B.J., where are we off to?"

She stopped and turned to stare up at him, shock causing her brows to soar. "We?"

"Yeah, I figured—"

"You figured," she snapped.

"Well, I thought—"

"No, you didn't, because if you had you would have remembered that I told you I work alone. Now," she spun around and began to walk away from him again, "good-bye, Marshal."

Mick felt his temper flare and his inseam tighten. What the hell was it about Miss B.J. bull-headed stubborn-as-all-get-out Poydras that caused his body and mind to dive into near lethal battle? He tried to count to ten, quit when he got to eight and she got out of his line of sight, and charged after her. Why couldn't she see that by using her knowledge of the city and his contacts with the local authorities, not to mention his expertise in investigating, they could work together and get this case solved in no time, rather than each going over the same ground separately?

He shoved open the door to the street and walked out, fully expecting to see B.J. getting into her car. Instead all he saw was an empty parking space.

Mick cursed silently. Before this case was over he'd be lucky if he wasn't thrown in jail for murdering her.

THREE

Beaujolais, who had been dropped off at B.J.'s condo earlier by Alice, greeted her at the door, bouncing happily and yipping a welcome.

She ruffled his head and gave him a cookie bone, which he promptly took out onto the balcony and lay down to eat.

B.J. tossed her jacket on a chair, walked into her bedroom, and threw herself onto the bed. The nerve of the man, following her like that. There was no law that said she had to cooperate with him, U.S. marshal or no U.S. marshal. It was a free country. She didn't have to work with him.

A frown tugged at her brow, and she rolled over and grabbed the phone from her nightstand. Dialing her office, B.J. heard the answering machine pick up, then punched another number to get her past the office greeting. "Alice, this is B.J. When you get to work in the morning, check around first thing and make certain there's no law that says I have to cooperate with a U.S. marshal." She hung up, replaced the phone, rolled onto her back, and stared up at the ceiling.

Anyway, they weren't really working the same case. Not technically. He was on the trail of some ex-con who might or might not have had some connection to Theodore Charbonneau—and she was more inclined to believe the latter. Blue bloods didn't usually associate with ex-cons. And anyway, she was just looking for Mrs. C.'s dog. Of course, finding Theodore alive could also mean finding the dog. B.J. sighed. But that was a ridiculous thought. Theodore Charbonneau was dead. Lying in the city morgue cold as a redfish.

She closed her eyes, and an image of Mick Gentry suddenly loomed forth to take over her thoughts. She couldn't argue, the man was sexy. In fact, that was probably the understatement of the year. If Adonis had ever really existed, Mick Gentry had to be his twin. And she'd always had a weak spot for blonds. She could almost feel his hard, muscled flesh beneath her fingers as they slid through the mat of golden hairs she just knew covered his chest. Each strand caressed her fingers like a thread of silk and . . .

B.J.'s eyes shot open and she bolted upright. "What in blazes am I doing?" she said into the silence. She shook her head, trying to rid her thoughts of their preoccupation with Mick Gentry, then shook her hands, her shoulders, and finally pushed herself off the bed and hurried into the bathroom. Ripping off her clothes, she stepped into the shower.

She'd never been man-crazy before, so what was the

matter with her now? He was good looking, yes, that was an undeniable fact. Actually, he was more than good looking, he was drop-dead gorgeous, and though she'd never thought much about scars before, the thin one on his lip seemed to accentuate his attractiveness rather than mar it.

"Oh, B.J., you're in trouble." She groaned, wrapping a towel around herself.

But she'd seen plenty of good-looking men in her time. New Orleans had more than its share. She'd even dated a few and had been engaged to three. So what was there about Mick Gentry that had her thoughts delving into erotic fantasy?

She stepped back into the bedroom just as the phone rang. Beaujolais barked. B.J. paused. Two rings later her answering machine clicked on and she waited, ready to pick up the receiver if the caller proved to be someone she wanted to talk to.

"B.J., ah, Miss Poydras, this is Mick Gentry. I, uh, thought we might meet somewhere for coffee and talk."

How had he gotten her home number? She was unlisted. B.J. glared at the machine as if it should give her the answer. She had no intention of going for coffee or anything else with Mick Gentry, yet something inside of her was urging B.J. to pick up the receiver and say yes. She hurriedly followed her first instinct. Without a backward glance at the phone, she spun on her heel and returned to the bathroom. "No, thanks, Marshal," she muttered over her shoulder.

She picked up her blow dryer and flicked it on, but

instead of the satisfying feeling she should have gotten at ignoring his call, she felt a little bit empty somehow.

Mick stared at the phone, then flipped it closed. She was there and just not answering his call. The woman was infuriating. Who ever heard of not cooperating with a U.S. marshal? Most people wouldn't even dare think about defying a marshal's request for cooperation, but then he was quickly coming to learn that B.J. Poydras wasn't most people.

"Thank heaven for small favors," he griped.

He glowered at the front door to her condo, restraining himself from walking across the street and pounding on it. He was being unprofessional, but then he'd skipped past that a while ago, when he'd cajoled her home phone number and address out of the desk sergeant at the Quarter's precinct. He'd lied and said they were working the case together and he needed to talk to her but had misplaced the piece of paper she'd written her number on for him. Of course there were any number of other ways he could have gotten the information, but that had looked to be the quickest and easiest. Doing this didn't sit well with him, but he was after Carl Townsend, and he'd do whatever was necessary to get the man. If that meant using B.J. Poydras, then he'd use B.J. Poydras.

But it would be nice if she'd be a little more cooperative about it. Mick slammed the gearshift knob into drive and pulled away from the curb.

38

The next morning Mick rose early and went directly to the police station, but the detective in charge of the Charbonneau case was out on a call. Two doughnuts and five cups of coffee later, Mick finally saw Dan Jarrett walk into the room. Jarrett waved, grabbed a cup of coffee, and walked to his desk, settling into his chair and looking at Mick, waiting for him to say something.

He did. "There's got to be a connection between Charbonneau and Townsend."

"Yeah, you said that before," Jarrett said, taking a gulp of his coffee. His nose wrinkled. "Damn, that stuff must have been sitting here since last night." He looked back at Mick. "Okay, let's say there's a connection. But they certainly weren't twins." The detective swiveled slightly in his chair, his black hair catching the sunbeams pouring in through a nearby window. Opening a drawer, he pulled out a photo of Theodore Charbonneau the NOPD had gotten from his wife and held it up next to a copy of the prison ID picture of Carl Townsend that Mick carried around with him. "I mean, hell, Gentry, Charbonneau was definitely not tall, dark, and handsome, but your guy Townsend is about as ugly as they come."

"Yeah, but there's a connection between them," Mick said again. "I'd bet on it. Charbonneau didn't report his credit card stolen—"

"Maybe he was the one who bought the ring."

Mick shook his head. "No, we know it was Townsend. And after Charbonneau left San Francisco and came back here, Townsend followed him."

Jarrett shook his head. "Sorry, I just don't see it, Gentry. Lillian Charbonneau's a blue blood, got ancestors that go back to the founding of this city, and my understanding is Charbonneau's family went back just as far up in Baton Rouge. What kind of connection would a man like that have with a career criminal like Townsend?"

Mick shrugged.

"None."

Both men looked up as the female voice invaded their conversation.

Mick groaned inwardly, then silently cursed as he watched B.J. Poydras walk toward him, her black and white dog, which looked more like a mutant mop bouncing across the floor, right behind her. She smiled, and Mick felt a subtle yet distinct physical change move through his body. His muscles seemed to get tighter, his temperature hotter, and the room suddenly seemed sucked dry of air and a whole lot smaller than it had only a few seconds earlier.

"What'dya want, Poydras?" Jarrett asked in a tone that said loud and clear that whatever it was she wanted, he probably wasn't feeling obliged to give it.

"Just wanted to check and see if you'd found Charbonneau's car yet."

Mick watched Beaujolais sniff Jarrett's leg as if he thought it was a fire hydrant.

"No." Jarrett shook his leg. "And get that mutt away from me."

B.J. smiled. "Okay, thanks. Come on, Beau." She turned and retraced her steps toward the door.

"That's it?" Jarrett called after her.

"That's it, *cheri.*" She threw her answer back over her shoulder.

"Umph. She usually wants a helluva lot more than that," Jarrett grumbled.

Mick watched her leave. He had pretty much decided that in spite of what he'd said to her the day he'd met her, playing her shadow wasn't going to get him anywhere. He was a professional, with contacts a lot better than hers, and he could solve the case of Charbonneau and Townsend on his own, the way he usually did. He had only gone to her in the first place because he'd thought it would save time and he'd suspected she might know something, because of being in with Mrs. Charbonneau, that he didn't. But he'd been wrong. He turned back to the detective. "I thought I'd go on over to Charbonneau's office and talk to his secretary. You got any problem with that?"

Jarrett shrugged. "Nah. Have a ball."

"Thanks."

The detective swiveled around in his chair as Mick started to walk away. "Hey, Marshal."

Mick paused and looked back. "Yeah?"

Jarrett rose and walked toward him, pausing only an inch away, and when he spoke it was barely above a whisper. "I can't check it out myself, politics and all that, you know," he raised his eyes upward, then looked back at Mick, "but scuttlebutt on the street has it that Little Jo Dubois had some kind of dealings with Charbonneau, and it didn't have anything to do with Charbonneau's regular business, if you know what I mean."

Mick grinned. "And just where might someone who doesn't give a damn about your local politics," he rolled his eyes upward, mocking Jarrett's earlier gesture, "find this Little Jo Dubois?"

"Well, Jo being the shady type of character that he is, if I was looking for him and was hoping he wasn't sleeping it off somewhere, I'd take me a stroll into a bar over on Bourbon called The Neon Magnolia."

"Thanks. I'll do that."

Mick decided to check out Little Jo before going to Charbonneau's office. It was still early in the day, but the bars in the Quarter never closed, which meant that to some people it was actually late.

Going to The Neon Magnolia was a mistake. The minute Mick walked into the dark interior of the place he sensed B.J.'s presence. He knew she was there. He didn't know how he knew, he just did.

Mick was just about to tell himself he was crazy when he heard her laugh. He blinked rapidly in an effort to adapt his eyes to the darkness, broken only by a large blue neon magnolia hanging over the bar, and several spotlights that pointed at a stripper doing her thing on a tiny stage toward the back of the room. Mick squinted into the murky darkness. "B.J.?"

A chair scraped across the floor. "Gentry? What are you doing here?"

A yip followed her question.

Mick turned and moved through the darkness, seeing B.J. and the man she was sitting with only a split second before walking into their table. "I could ask you the same thing," he said, staring down at her.

"You came to talk to Little Jo."

Mick sat down. "Yeah, how'd you know?"

B.J. turned to the man sitting next to her. "Mick Gentry," she said, "meet Little Jo Dubois."

The man was wearing dark glasses. He was also wearing a tank top, revealing arms bigger than most people's thighs and bulging pecs lying atop a mound of stomach. A pair of wool gloves lay before him on the table, and his head was covered with a stocking cap. Two thoughts instantly tramped through Mick's mind: First, that Little Jo was a far cry from being little, and second, that either the man was having a hard time deciding if it was winter or summer, or he was just plain crazy.

Mick stuck out his hand and Little Jo looked at it as if he thought it was a snake ready to attack him.

"You a cop?" he snarled.

B.J.'s foot rammed into Mick's shin. "No," he said, which wasn't a total lie. He wasn't a cop, he was a U.S. marshal. Some people didn't see a difference. He did.

"Private?" Little Jo persisted.

"He's working with me," B.J. said.

Little Jo looked at her. "He helping you find—"

"Yeah, right," she said hurriedly, cutting him off. "He's helping me." She rose and palmed Little Jo a bill.

Mick couldn't see how much she gave him.

"Thanks, Little Jo. You put out the word to your guys, and if you hear anything, let me know right away, okay?"

"Sho', honey. We see that little monster anywhere, you'll be the first to know."

"And you'll check the black market dealers—" B.J. stopped and glanced at Mick, instantly wishing she hadn't

Tricks of the Trade

said that. Now he'd want to know what she wanted Little Jo to check the black market dealers for. Drat.

"Minute you leave," Little Jo said. "My boys'll be on it. Minute you leave."

She nodded, scooped Beaujolais up and into her arms, and turned toward the door.

"Little monster?" Mick echoed as he followed her out onto the street. "What was that all about? I thought Charbonneau was supposed to be such an upstanding citizen."

"He was." B.J. walked between two parked cars and headed for her own across the street.

"Then how come your friend in there called him a little monster? What, Charbonneau have some kind of secret sadistic habit or something?"

"Or something," she said, opening her car door. Beaujolais jumped into the passenger seat, and B.J. slid into the driver's seat and shut the door in Mick's face.

Minutes later, after watching her drive away, he gave up trying to count to one hundred and reconciled himself to the fact that B.J. Poydras had the uncanny and annoying ability to push him from calm to furious in one second flat. He climbed into his own car, flipped open his cellular phone, and called NOPD. "Jarrett," he growled into the mouthpiece after being transferred to the detective's line and hearing him answer, "I need you to get me the names of any black market dealers you know of operating out of the French Quarter."

"Black market for what?" Jarrett answered. "They do specialize, you know."

"Anything Theodore Charbonneau might have wanted to sell or trade. Whatever. Check them all."

"Cripes, Gentry, that could have been anything. And what makes you think Charbonneau was dealing in the black market anyway?"

"Suspicion. And right now that's all I've got to go on, so don't ask any more questions, just do it, okay? I'll call you back in an hour."

Mick drove to Charbonneau's office, which was located on Canal Street, a wide thoroughfare that acted as the northwest boundary separating the Quarter from the more modern business district.

From his immediate impression of Charbonneau's secretary, Mick guessed that she'd most likely been hired more because of the way she filled out a dress rather than due to any great talent with a computer. But whatever Charbonneau's reason had been, Mick appreciated the view.

"I'm sorry." She flipped her long blond hair over her shoulder and looked up at him. "Mr. Charbonneau is—"

"I know," Mick said. "Dead." He looked down at her from beneath the Stetson, pushed back the right side of his jacket so that she could see his badge, and held out his ID. "I'm Mick Gentry, U.S. Marshal. And you are?"

"Oh, I've never met a U.S. marshal before." She smiled coyly and leaned slightly forward, giving him a better view of the cleavage peeking out from the neckline of a blouse that was already very revealing. "How exciting. Are you like Wyatt Earp or something? I just love cowboys. You're all so big and strong."

"Yeah, we do our best. Now if you could—"

Tricks of the Trade

"You're not here to arrest Mr. Arnold, are you?"

"Ah, no. Who's Mr. Arnold?"

"Oh, he's taking over things for Mr. Charbonneau." She sniffed appropriately, then looked back up at him and smiled. "I'm Bobbi Delanoi. If you've come to see Mr. Arnold, I'm afraid you can't. He's in a meeting."

"Actually I came to see you, Bobbi. What can you tell me about Charbonneau?"

She smiled like a cat who definitely knew the difference between milk and cream and was used to getting the cream. "He was very generous."

"Um, like with time off, that kind of thing?"

"Well, yes, that, and like, well . . ." She held out her arm, wrist cocked downward. "He gave me this gold bracelet for being here a year." She fingered her necklace. "And this for my birthday."

Mick looked at the gold necklace and wondered what extra little secretarial duties Bobbi had performed to merit the jewelry. "Were you . . . did you see Mr. Charbonneau socially, Bobbi?" he asked, realizing he could get a slap across the face just as easily as an answer for his bluntness.

"We just went to lunch together," she said.

Mick nodded. Must have been some real nice lunches, he surmised. He questioned her for the next half hour, then decided that was long enough. What he came away with was a headache and the conviction that the woman couldn't make up her mind if she was trying to imitate Marilyn Monroe, Farrah Fawcett, or Jayne Mansfield, but in his opinion she had a ways to go with her act. And if she'd been having an affair with Charbonneau, she wasn't copping to it.

He got a flash of satisfaction when the elevator doors opened and he came face to face with B.J. Poydras. The feeling was gone as quickly as it had come over him when he realized that while he'd been talking to Charbonneau's secretary and finding out virtually nothing, B.J. had been somewhere else, talking to someone else, and he had no idea where or whom.

"Hello, Marshal," B.J. said coolly, and brushed past him.

"She doesn't know anything," he called after her.

B.J. paused and looked back. A sly smile slowly tugged the corners of her lips upward. "Maybe she just doesn't want to tell you."

"And maybe she doesn't know anything."

B.J. shrugged and disappeared into Charbonneau's office.

Mick felt attacked by an uncomfortable snugness in his jeans and he tugged at their inseam. It didn't help. He turned back to the elevator and saw that the doors had closed. "Terrific." He jabbed a thumb on the button again.

By the time he got to the ground floor Mick had decided he wanted to know just what B.J. Poydras was asking Bobbi Delanoi. Or more to the point, what Bobbi was saying to B.J. He pushed the button for Charbonneau's floor and the elevator began its ascent. A minute later he was in front of Bobbi's desk and B.J. was nowhere in sight.

"The private detective who was here, she left already?"

Bobbi nodded. "She was probably going down while you were coming up."

"What'd she want to know?"

Bobbi frowned. "Excuse me?"

Mick slid a hip onto the corner of her desk and smiled his most flirtatious smile. "What did she ask you?"

Bobbi smiled back. "Same kind of things you did." She glanced at a clock on the wall, then looked back at Mick with a wicked gleam in her eye. "It's almost lunch time, Marshal. Why don't we discuss this at the café downstairs? Or better yet, I could take the afternoon off and we could . . ." She let the insinuation hang in the air.

Mick surprised himself by ignoring the blatant invitation, and realizing, with a bit of annoyance, that he'd been subconsciously comparing her to B.J. Bobbi wasn't coming up too good in the comparison. "Did she ask you anything different than I did?"

"No, she . . . well, she did ask about ChiChi."

He stood abruptly. "ChiChi? What's ChiChi?"

Bobbi laughed. "Not what. Who. He's Mrs. Charbonneau's poodle. Mr. Charbonneau used to bring him to the office sometimes, when his wife was out of town or something."

Mick was puzzled. "What did Miss Poydras want to know about the dog?"

"Who walked him, took care of him when Mr. Charbonneau was busy, that kind of thing. Why?"

"And who did?"

Bobbi sighed, as if exasperated with all the questions. "Jeffy."

"Jeffy who?"

"Jefferson Marville. He works in the mailroom."

Mick turned to go.

"He's not here today."

Mick paused and looked back at her. "So, where is he?"

"Called in sick, poor thing."

"Yeah, poor thing," Mick agreed. "What's Marville's address?"

Bobbi retrieved a purse from beneath her desk. She flashed a smile at Mick again. "Well, shall we get that lunch now?"

"I'd love to, Bobbi, but I really can't today. Sorry." He wasn't going to say he'd call another time, because he had no intention of doing so. "I'll make it up to you, though." He smiled, letting her decipher what his words meant. "But before you go, could you tell me where this Jefferson Marville lives?"

"Yeah, in that creepy old Lalaurie mansion in the Quarter." She feigned a shiver to emphasize her distaste of Jeffy's home location. "The house is supposed to be haunted by all the servants Mrs. Lalaurie killed there back in the 1800s, when it was still a mansion, before they turned the place into apartments. Jeffy even swears he's seen them, the ghosts." A forced laugh slipped from her throat. "I don't believe him, but I sure wouldn't live there."

"Yeah, me neither. Thanks, Bobbi."

"Call me now, y'hear," she said, and winked. "And make it up to me."

B.J. had never been inside the Lalaurie house. She knew its history—everyone who lived in New Orleans knew its sordid history. But it was just one part of a collage of weird things that had transpired in New Orleans way back when. Delphine Lalaurie had held many grand parties in her French Quarter house in the early 1800s, but her wealth and generosity were not enough to squelch the rumors that her slaves were being tortured and some had committed suicide to avoid it. Then one night she was giving a dinner party and the house caught fire. As friends and neighbors rushed to help put out the fire, they found starving and tortured slaves chained to the attic walls. While her house burned and the authorities struggled to free the slaves, Delphine Lalaurie fled the scene in her carriage, never to be seen or heard of again.

The house wasn't open to tours now because it had been cut into apartments, though why anyone would live there was beyond B.J.'s understanding. Not only did the place have a horrible story attached to it, but most of the old-timers swore it was haunted by the souls of Lalaurie's victims. And it was desperately in need of repair.

She walked up the stairs, Beaujolais at her heels. B.J. held tight to the banister and tried to ignore the loudly creaking wood beneath her feet. She suddenly pictured the stairs collapsing beneath her and sending her plunging downward. B.J. pushed aside the horrid vision, stepped around the railing, and stopped in front of apartment 4B.

Beaujolais practically hugged her ankle, a little whimper escaping his throat every few seconds. B.J. knocked on the door, but it was the one behind her that opened. She turned and saw an extremely skinny young man with long brown hair and a mouth full of something, sticking his face out at her.

"Who are you?" he asked, chewing at the same time he spoke.

"A friend of Jeffy's," B.J. said, hoping Mr. Skeleton didn't know all of Jeffy's friends.

"I've never seen you before."

Beaujolais barked, as if getting his courage back.

"Or the mutt either."

"Well, we've never seen you before either," B.J. countered.

The skeleton smiled. "Got me there." He crammed another wad of something into his mouth and through it said, "Well, he's down in the courtyard."

"Thanks." She went back downstairs and walked through a large, dimly lit, musky smelling room that she guessed at one time might have been a parlor. A pair of French doors stood open, and through them she could see the courtyard. As she approached the doorway B.J. saw that the courtyard was just as badly in need of repair and maintenance as the building.

A piercing scream suddenly broke the otherwise peaceful silence.

B.J. stopped abruptly. Her heart jumped into her throat and she grabbed the doorjamb.

Tricks of the Trade

Beaujolais cowered at her feet and snarled.

Chills raced up B.J.'s back as she looked up, fully expecting to see a body hurtling from the roof. Instead all she saw was blue sky and the surrounding walls of the building.

She looked about, confused, and saw a young man sitting on a wooden bench located in the center of the courtyard. He was reading a book, seemingly concentrating deeply on it, as if he hadn't heard a thing. B.J. looked up toward the roof again, at the ground, then back at the man who she assumed was Jeffy. Maybe he was deaf. She walked toward him, thoroughly bewildered. "Excuse me, but someone just screamed," she said, not knowing what else to say and still worried that someone was hurt somewhere.

"Yeah, I know." He didn't bother to look up. "But it's okay. She's dead."

FOUR

B.J.'s mouth dropped open as she stared at Jefferson Marville. "Dead?"

He looked up, blew his nose, and smiled. "Yeah. Who are you?"

"What do you mean dead?"

"Dead. You know, no pulse, no heartbeat." He chuckled softly. "No body. You know, lady, d-e-a-d, dead."

"I don't get it." She felt as if she was unwittingly participating in an Abbott and Costello routine. "Who's dead? Where?"

"The ghost, lady, the ghost." He seemed a little exasperated with her now.

B.J.'s head whipped around, and she stared up at the roof. "A ghost. Here?"

He nodded. "Yeah. Supposedly she threw herself off the roof way back when to keep from being tortured. She was a slave."

B.J. looked around. "And she just did it again?"

"Yep. She does it every day about this time."

B.J. looked back at him. "Really?"

He nodded. "Guess once wasn't enough." A wide grin split his face. "So, are you a tourist, or here to rent an apartment? Or did Elsie just change your mind for you?"

"Elsie?"

He put his book down. "The ghost. That's what a few of us who live here call her." He shrugged. "I don't know who started it, but it stuck. There's also James, a butler. He roams the halls at night trying to serve tea. And Sarah Lee. We figure she was a cook 'cause we only see her in what used to be the old kitchen area."

B.J. felt a shiver run up her spine. "I'm, ah, B.J. Poydras, and I'm here to ask you . . . wait, you are Jefferson Marville, aren't you?"

He nodded. "In the flesh." A cough burst from his lips, as if to confirm the statement. "Sorry, nasty cold."

"I have a few questions about Mr. Charbonneau's dog, if you don't mind."

"Too bad about Charbonneau." Jeffy shook his head. "ChiChi's a cute little mutt though."

"He's a purebred poodle, not a mutt."

"Yeah, well, whatever he is, I used to take him walking. And he was always running off, you know? Scooting under one bush or another, chasing kids, squirrels, birds, whatever. But he always looked so ridiculous with that fluffed up pom-pom haircut he had."

"Where else did you take him?"

He frowned. "What do you mean?"

"Groomers, pet stores, the local coffeehouse, a friend's?" She was losing her patience and getting snippy, but hearing a ghost scream while it jumped off a roof in the middle of the day could do that to a person. Especially when someone told you that the house you had to walk back through in order to leave had a few more otherworldly inhabitants lurking in it.

"Oh, well, every so often Mr. Charbonneau would have me take ChiChi to Lucille's. That was when he was going to be out for most of the day and I had to get some work done. Deliver the mail and all that."

"Lucille's. What's that? A dog groomer?"

He nodded. "She runs a place on Canal, right off Royale. Grooming, animal sitting, pet shop. I'd take ChiChi in there and drop her off, and Lu would watch her till I came back."

"Thanks," B.J. said. "You've been a big help."

"Yeah? But what's ChiChi and Lu got to do with the boss's death?"

"I'm not sure yet. Probably nothing. Come on, Beau," B.J. said, scooping up the dog. She turned and hurried from the courtyard, walking briskly through the house, eyes looking straight ahead, shoulders stiff. She didn't want to see or hear any more ghosts, and from the way Beaujolais huddled against her, she guessed he didn't either.

Once back on the banquette she turned and looked up at the house again.

"Pretty bizarre, huh?"

B.J. nearly jumped out of her skin at hearing Mick's voice behind her. Spinning around, she glared at him, seeing her own reflection staring back at her from the silver lenses of his sunglasses. "Don't do that!"

Mick's brows rose above the glasses. "Do what?"

She gasped in an effort to catch her breath again.

His car was parked directly behind her own, and he was leaning on its front bumper, legs crossed at the ankles, thumbs hooked into the belt loops of his jeans. The Stetson sat on the car's hood.

He looked good. Totally appetizing. B.J. slammed a lid down on her traitorous thoughts. "Never mind," she snapped. "Just stop following me."

Beaujolais jumped to the ground and trotted over to sniff Mick's boot.

B.J. dug into her bag for her car keys, refusing to acknowledge to herself that upon seeing him her pulse had shifted into overdrive and her heart had begun beating like a tom-tom. Nor was she willing to admit that there was any reason for her physical upheaval other than that he'd startled her.

"I wasn't following you," Mick said.

"Oh, you just happen to show up everywhere I go by accident, is that it, Marshal?"

He shook his head, and a curl of blond hair fell onto his forehead.

B.J. wanted to reach out and touch it, then silently cursed herself.

He swiped at the wayward lock of hair, pushing it back into place, and grinned at B.J. "Yes and no. I'm ending up everywhere you do because we're both working the same case, remember? As for showing up about the same time as you, that's probably more or less coincidental."

"I'll bet."

He grinned. "You'd lose. I got to Charbonneau's secretary first, remember?"

"Look, I don't know how many different ways to say this, Marshal. We are not working the same case. I'm working for Mrs. Charbonneau, you're looking for some escaped con named Townsend. They're different cases. Not related. Totally unconnected. Understand?"

His grin didn't disappear, and he didn't make any move to leave. Several very unladylike, unspeakable curses danced through B.J.'s mind. She had no intention of telling him that she knew it was impossible for their cases to have anything to do with each other because he was hunting an escaped convict and she was looking for a dog. That she wasn't looking for Theodore Charbonneau, wasn't trying to discover if he was alive rather than dead.

Of course, confessing what her real case was to Mick Gentry might get him to leave her alone, but it was humiliating enough having to admit to herself that she was playing pet detective. She certainly had no intention of letting anyone else know. If word got out, she'd be the laughingstock of the police department, not to mention every other P.I. in the city.

Besides, he was distracting her from business, making her think about things she didn't need to be thinking about.

"What'd you find out from Jeffy?"

B.J. fumed. He wasn't going to stop. He was going to hound her every step until he drove her nuts. Jerking open the door of her car, B.J. shot Mick her best "I wish you'd go away and never come back" look.

He continued to smile.

For a split second she wondered what it would be like to feel his lips on hers. The thought was the straw that broke the camel's back. "Go talk to him yourself," she snapped. "Oh, and by the way," B.J. paused halfway into her car and gave him a saucy smile. "I'm going back to my office now, Marshal," she said, her tone dripping sarcasm, "just in case you want to follow me. We wouldn't want you to get lost."

"Thanks. But I never do."

She gunned the motor and took off, leaving rubber from her tires on the pavement. It made her cringe thinking about all the mileage she'd sacrificed. Stupid. But then handsome men sometimes made her do stupid things. Especially, handsome, infuriating men.

The realization made her temper boil all the more.

Mick watched her drive away, but he didn't move. Not because he didn't want to, but because he couldn't. Or rather, knew he shouldn't. Not until his body calmed down. For some reason he was at a total loss to explain or understand, B.J. Poydras could turn his body into a throbbing, simmering mass of desire. And she wasn't even trying—that was the part that really got to him.

She wasn't his type either. Short, sassy, and dark, with eyes that dared him to do just about anything, a tongue he knew she must sharpen every night, and a chip on her shoulder that had to weigh a ton. He preferred tall, lithe women with long graceful limbs and bodies that moved like cats. And his tastes usually ran to blondes. Sometimes even redheads. He liked a woman to be a woman: feminine, sexy, and soft. Not all spit and sass.

Sherry had been sexy and soft—until that day.

Mick pushed the memory of his ex-wife from his mind, but before he could prevent it, thoughts of B.J. zoomed back in to take over. He didn't know why he was attracted to her. She was everything he normally didn't like, and that went way beyond the physical. She was pushy, stubborn, and aggressive, worked in a man's world, doing a man's job, and except for an occasional spark of something in her eyes when she looked at him that might or might not be desire, she hadn't given him one ounce of encouragement in that direction.

So what was his problem? It wasn't as if he *really* needed her on the case. Her cooperation would have made things a little easier, maybe answered some of the questions nagging at him about the connection between Charbonneau and Townsend, but he didn't really *need* her. He didn't *need* anyone.

Mick finally straightened and entered Jeffy's building. He paused in what was supposed to be the lobby and looked around. Once, he sensed, it had been the grand foyer of a townhouse that had been furnished with only the best of everything. Mick felt a touch of sadness as his gaze moved over the cracking walls, faded wallpaper, and a floor badly in need of repair.

A young man entered from another door, the end of his nose red, his eyes glassy. "Can I help you?"

"I'm looking for Jeff Marville."

"I'm Jeffy."

Mick automatically pushed back his jacket to reveal his badge and retrieved his wallet, flipping it open so Jeffy could see his ID. "What can you tell me about Theodore Charbonneau?"

Jeffy moaned. "That lady was just in here asking questions. Wasn't she with you?"

"No. What'd you tell her?"

"That I took ChiChi for walks for Mr. Charbonneau, and sometimes to Lucille's if Mr. Charbonneau was going to be gone most of the day."

"ChiChi? Lucille?" Mick echoed. "Who are they?"

Jeffy rolled his eyes. "Wow, don't you guys ever talk to each other?" He sighed, patted a tissue to his nose, winced, and finally explained. "ChiChi is Mrs. Charbonneau's dog, and Lucille was the pet sitter who took care of him when Mr. Charbonneau brought the mutt to the office 'cause his wife was out of town and I was too busy to do it. He always expected me to do something with the dog, but sometimes I had my own work to do, you know? So I'd take him to Lu's and she'd watch him. You know, keep him out of the way."

"That's it?" Mick asked, surprised. "That's all you told Miss Poydras?"

He shrugged. "That's all she asked about."

"Is there more?"

Jeffy shrugged again. "Like what?"

"Mr. Charbonneau ever have any unusual clients come to the office? People that seemed not the type he would be associating with, anything like that?"

"Ummm, not really, unless you count the women."

"Women?"

"Yeah, he was always playing around with somebody, you know? He especially liked the strippers from Bourbon Street. I think he knew some of the club owners and that's how he met the girls. I don't think they liked him all that much, but they liked his money, you know?"

Mick smiled. So, Charbonneau had some lady friends. Maybe one of them knew what the connection between him and Townsend was. Maybe one of them was the connection. Maybe even knew where Townsend was hiding. Mick wondered if this had any connection to Little Jo Dubois. "Any one lady in particular come around a lot?"

Jeffy shrugged. "I dunno. They all kinda look alike to me." He raised his hands in front of his chest as if he were gripping something. "You know?"

Mick nodded and glanced at his watch. He hadn't had anything to eat all day except the doughnuts and coffee he'd pilfered at the police station, and it was nearing dinnertime. He thanked Jeffy, left, and headed for his hotel. Halfway there he changed his mind. For some reason he didn't like the idea that B.J. Poydras was ticked at him. He knew he shouldn't care, but he did.

"Professional courtesy," he said to himself. "That's all it is." Pulling up to the drive-up window of a fast food restaurant, Mick ordered enough for three people. Seconds later he pulled into another fast food joint down the street from the first and rattled off another order. He repeated the process two more times. Once his front seat was full of neatly contained food he drove toward B.J.'s office, all the while trying to ignore the slow heat that had started to build in his body.

Tricks of the Trade

61

B.J. had turned away from the window and walked back to her desk when the intercom buzzed. After leaving Jeffy's she'd stopped at the address he'd given her for Lucille's Pet Grooming Salon and Boarding House, but the woman, a dowdy little old lady who wore a baseball cap, had offered nothing helpful. She said she knew ChiChi, liked the dog, and bemoaned the fact that with Mr. Charbonneau dead, even if the dog was found, she'd probably never see ChiChi again or the $75 she usually charged for sitting him. B.J. got the distinct impression that it was more the $75 the old lady was going to miss than the dog.

Upon her return to the office she'd rechecked with the animal shelters and adoption agencies, even though Alice had done it twice that day already, but she struck out with them too. Since then she'd been trying to figure out what her next move should be and *not* think about Mick Gentry. B.J. picked up the phone. "Yes, Alice?"

"There's someone here to see you and, ah, he's got dinner."

"Dinner?"

"Uh-huh."

"Not the Marshal."

The words were barely out of her mouth when the door to her office opened and he walked in. She didn't even know why she'd thought it was him, other than the fact that she knew it wouldn't have been any of her ex-fiancés and she wasn't dating anyone. But it wasn't wishful thinking, she told herself quickly. No, more like dread. B.J. hung up the phone as he strode toward her carrying a large box and a couple of bags.

Beaujolais danced around Mick's feet, his nose wiggling a mile a minute as the odors of various foods caught his attention.

"Marshal, I'm sorry you went to this trouble," B.J. said, glancing at Beaujolais and wanting to call him a traitor, "but this just won't work."

Glancing past his shoulder, she saw Alice standing in the doorway, the grin of a Cheshire cat on her face. *Make that two traitors.*

Mick plopped his cache on her desk. "I didn't know what you liked," he said, "so I got a bit of everything. Kind of."

Beaujolais jumped onto one of the chairs facing B.J.'s desk and, sniffing frantically, yipped.

B.J. ignored him and looked at Mick. "Marshal Gentry, I appreciate the gesture, but I've still got a lot of work to do tonight, and I'm really not that hungry." Actually, now that the smell of food was wafting under her nose, she realized she was starving, but the last thing she wanted to do was have a cozy little dinner in her office with *him*. And she really didn't have any work to do. In fact, she'd just been thinking about going home when he'd arrived. "Look, I've got a case to solve and—"

"And you've got to eat."

"No, really, I—" Her stomach picked that inopportune time to growl.

"See?" Amusement flickered in his eyes and an easy smile pulled at his lips.

B.J. felt like melting and steeled herself against the urge.

"Sounds like the mop could use something to eat

too," he said, and chuckled. "Now, I've got fried chicken, hamburgers . . . one of which we can give to him," Mick said, glancing at Beaujolais, "some gumbo, cornbread, biscuits, salad." He retrieved a box that had been packed under the others and held it up. "And . . ." A devilish gleam replaced the glint of amusement in his eyes. "Chocolate cake. All you need to provide is soda and coffee."

B.J. groaned. Chocolate was her downfall. She glanced past Mick's broad shoulders and toward her secretary. B.J. had a sneaking suspicion that the marshal had received a little helping hand with his scheme, but Alice was just disappearing out the door to the hall. "Sodas are in the bar," she called out, "and I made a fresh pot of coffee a little while ago." She waved good-bye before B.J. could say anything.

"I figured after our argument earlier I owed you an apology," Mick said as he opened containers and set out the food.

She eyed him suspiciously. Something told her there was a lot more to this so-called peace offering than that. "Thank you, but I'm still not working with you."

He shrugged and handed her a paper plate, then broke up one of the hamburgers and set it on another plate on the floor for Beaujolais.

Beau practically dived into the food.

Mick sat down, his own plate already loaded with food. "Looks like I was right, he was hungry."

"He's always hungry," B.J. grumbled, spooning coleslaw onto her plate. She paused and looked at Mick. "I mean it, Marshal, I'm not going to change my mind about working with you."

"I think Charbonneau had a girlfriend."

B.J. stopped with a spoon of coleslaw in midair. "A girlfriend? How do you know? I haven't heard anything like that."

He smiled, and a delicious shiver raced up B.J.'s spine. No, she wasn't going to go there, she told herself. It was too dangerous.

"Maybe you just didn't ask the right kind of question," Mick said.

She fought down the insidious feelings he had managed to arouse in her. Okay, so she wasn't immune to him, but she had no intention of allowing herself to fall under his spell.

"Or maybe it was just a guy thing," Mick said. "You know, something a guy only feels comfortable telling another guy about his boss."

B.J. forced her brain to work, her thoughts to get back to the case. "Jeffy told you Mr. Charbonneau had a girlfriend?" She felt like zipping back to Jeffy Marville's apartment and dropping her coleslaw over his head.

"Well, not exactly. He said the old guy liked women, especially strippers. So maybe he didn't have *a* girlfriend. Maybe he had a lot of them." His chuckle was dry and cynical.

"Did Jeffy have any names?"

"Ah, no."

"Well, it doesn't change anything anyway," B.J. said, shrugging. "Probably doesn't even mean anything."

"You know," Mick said as he picked up a piece of

chicken, "you have to be the stubbornest woman I've ever met. Beautiful, but stubborn as hell." He nearly choked on his chicken at hearing his own words. Why in the hell had he said that bit about her being beautiful? It was true, but that didn't mean he'd had to say it.

Since she didn't know how to take a compliment wedged within what she considered an insult, B.J. decided to ignore it, but that didn't prevent a blush from creeping its hot little way over her cheeks. She tried to sound cool, calm, and collected when she responded. "I know you feel our cases are intertwined somehow, Marshal, but . . ."

"Mick."

"Excuse me?"

He smiled. "My name's Mick."

B.J. stared at him for a long moment, trying to steel herself against the onslaught of his smile. He's a cop, she reminded herself. And he didn't want to help her, he wanted to use her. "As I was saying, *Marshal* . . ."

What little patience he'd managed to hang on to deserted him at her haughty tone. "I know what you were saying, Miss Poydras, and you're wrong. You're looking for Charbonneau, I'm looking for Townsend, and I know there's a connection between the two. The way I see it, if we find one guy, we're very likely to find a lead on the other." He leaned forward. "So what the hell is your problem, *Miz* Poydras? Why don't you want to make life easy for both of us and work with me on this thing?" One brow cocked skyward. "Or don't you like men?"

What in blazes was he doing? The hurt that flashed in her eyes at his last remark made him feel like a heel. A heel is exactly what Sherry had called him toward the end, so it was probably true that he was a heel. Nevertheless, he hadn't meant to jump down B.J.'s throat. He'd intended to cajole her into a good mood if she wasn't already in one. He'd intended to sweet-talk her, charm her, reason with her, and make her see they could stop tripping over each other if she would just stop being so stubborn. He was willing to bet his last dollar that Charbonneau was connected with Townsend, but since using the normal channels had produced nothing, and the man's so-called widow wouldn't talk to him, Mick knew B.J. was his best bet.

His intentions had been good; the fact that his body was turning into an inferno as he sat watching her was not.

"I'm stubborn?" she snapped, slamming her plastic fork down.

Startled, Beaujolais jumped up and barked. Neither paid him any attention.

"I've got a problem?" B.J. glowered at Mick. "How many times have I said I wouldn't work with you, Marshal? Two? Three? A half dozen? Yet you keep following me around trying to get me to change my mind."

Mick opened his mouth to reply but didn't get a chance.

"I thought marshals worked alone, did their own thing. Isn't that what you said? You've got all the newest equipment at your disposal, all the latest information. What do you need me for?"

"Most people would—"

"I'm not most people," B.J. said, cutting him off. "And for your information, Marshal Gentry, I've been engaged three times in the past five years, so I definitely do like men, I just don't like you!"

He opened his mouth, then slammed it shut before anything came out. She was the damnedest woman he'd ever met, and he'd probably be much better off if he walked away from her right now and never looked back.

FIVE

Of course Mick had no intention of leaving, which he figured probably meant he had a whole lot less sense than he'd always assumed he had.

"You're probably right," he said, deciding to change his tactics and barely stifling a laugh at the surprised look that came over B.J.'s face at his words. "There's most likely no real connection between our cases. After all, I'm looking for an escaped convict, and you're only trying to verify that a guy is dead so his widow can collect his insurance money." He shrugged, knowing he was purposely baiting her and unable to stop himself. "I mean, who would be ludicrous enough to want to add a lot of intrigue and danger to such an easy, no-brainer case?" Mick smiled. "Not me."

"No-brainer case?" Indignation swept through her like fire through dry kindling. If there had been anything on her desk she didn't mind destroying, she would have thrown it at him. Her hands clenched into fists. He was trying to provoke her. She knew it and she knew he knew it. "You don't know the first thing about my case."

He smiled widely. "Sure I do." Mick stared at her for several seconds, trying to figure out what he was doing and why. Normally if someone refused to cooperate with him, which wasn't very often, he just went around them. Or over them. If he wanted to, he could have her license yanked, her business canceled, even her dog snatched by the dogcatcher. So why was he tap-dancing with B.J. Poydras?

The thought that he wouldn't mind having her in his bed for a couple of hours skittered across his consciousness and didn't do anything to cool the ardor already simmering in his veins.

"See, I said you didn't know what you were talking about," B.J. said, interrupting his thoughts and jerking him back to reality.

Pushing his fantasy aside, Mick rose to her challenge. "Mrs. Charbonneau hired you to figure out what happened to her husband and, since the coroner is taking his sweet time verifying it's really him lying in the morgue, and the local cops aren't going to do any more investigating until someone tells them they have to, she wants you to do it so she can collect the insurance money and be done with it." He grinned. "Satisfied?"

A smirk pulled at one corner of her lips. "No. That's not what—" She snapped her mouth closed, suddenly realizing she had been about to tell him her case didn't involve finding Mr. Charbonneau.

Half finished with a hamburger, Mick ignored B.J.'s sudden silence. He set his plate down and pushed himself out of his chair, then walked to the far side of the room. "This thing work?" he asked over his shoulder.

"Yes."

He flipped on the small stereo that B.J. had installed in the office for nights when she worked late. Music always soothed her nerves, and sometimes even let her concentrate better. She nearly groaned in self-defeat when a very slow, very sensuous tune filled the room.

Mick turned and walked to stand before the large window that looked out onto Jackson Square. "I always wondered what Mardi Gras was like," he said softly.

B.J. got up from her chair and moved to stand beside him, telling herself it wasn't because she wanted to, but because she didn't like anyone standing behind her.

He remained silent, so she turned her attention to the scene beyond the window. Darkness had fallen over the city while they'd eaten, creeping steadily and silently over everything like a stealthy black cat, then settling down for a long, cozy slumber. The streetlights around the now almost deserted Jackson Square gave off a soft glow, while across from the square's main entrance the lights of the Café DuMonde lit up the banquette of Decatur Street, and the riverboat *Natchez* sounded its whistle as it pulled away from the wharf, its huge red paddle wheel slowly churning the dark waters.

"Most everyone is over on Rue Royale for the parade."

He nodded, but B.J. had the distinct impression that he was a million miles away.

"Sometimes," he said softly, contradicting her assumption, "when I'm in a place with a lot of history I look

Tricks of the Trade

out at it at night and try to imagine what it was like a hundred years or so ago."

B.J. started, surprised, then stared up at him. "I wouldn't have expected you . . . I mean, a U.S. marshal to be a , ah . . . romantic."

Mick shrugged. "I'm not, according to my ex-wife."

B.J. started again, wondering, and hating herself for it, if that was regret she heard in his voice.

"Where's home, Marshal?" she asked, suddenly wanting to change the subject.

He turned to her, a faraway look in his eyes. "A small ranch in Nevada. Just outside of Reno."

"A real cowboy, huh?"

He looked back out onto the square. "Sometimes, when I'm home, I sit out on my front porch and look out at the desert and listen to the quiet."

"Sounds kind of lonely."

Mick smiled. "You should try it sometime. Might surprise yourself." The moment he said it, he tensed at the realization that it sounded like a subtle invitation . . . and inviting B.J. Poydras to his ranch was about the last thing he wanted to do. That was his place, a sanctuary where he could be himself and be alone with his thoughts. He'd invite her into his bed, yes. To his home, no.

The last thought surprised him, since he hadn't really been aware he'd actually decided he wanted to take her to his bed. Yet there was no way he could deny the magnetism that had been building between them ever since they'd met, and he knew she felt it too. His fingers suddenly ached to reach out and touch her.

"You know," B.J. said, feeling the allure between

them building to an uncomfortably dangerous point, "it really would be better if we did work together." It was a second before she realized what she'd said. No, her mind screamed. She'd said the exact opposite of what she'd meant to say. B.J. opened her mouth to refute her statement, then realized she'd sound like a fool. Turning away, she resettled herself in her chair. How could she have done that?

Startled by her sudden change of mind, Mick hurriedly sat back into his own chair before she could look at him and get a glimpse of where his thoughts had really been. He smiled. "So, what changed your mind?"

B.J. started shuffling some papers on her desk. She'd done it, now she'd have to make the best of it. "Well, I was thinking about how we kept running into each other today, and that you were right, that's a waste of time." Actually what she'd been thinking was that she desperately wanted to know what it would feel like to be held in his arms and kissed. She'd had the distinct impression, while they'd been standing by the window, that if she didn't move, didn't get away from him, she was going to find out. The thought had almost pushed her into panic. She forced herself to continue. "But, if you've changed your mind about it, I guess that's . . ."

"No, you just surprised me, that's all," Mick said, ordering his body to calm down and his mind to return to business. Which he found, to his dismay, was easier said than done.

For the next hour they talked about the case. Mick again told B.J. all the reasons that had him convinced Charbonneau and Townsend were connected somehow.

She listened and ad-libbed, telling a fib here, an outright lie there, with absolutely no intention of telling him the truth of why Mrs. Charbonneau had hired her.

Anyway, she reasoned to herself, if they found Theodore Charbonneau alive, they would most likely find ChiChi, or if they proved it was Theodore in the morgue, she was no worse off than now. And along the way, even if the man was indeed dead, as she and everyone else except maybe Marshal Gentry believed, they might get a lead on where he'd dumped ChiChi.

Mick's escaped convict might have the dog, might even be planning to blackmail Mrs. Charbonneau for it, though if that was the case B.J. had to wonder why the man hadn't already made his ransom demand. And if they worked together, B.J. reasoned further, she wouldn't have a shadow anymore. They could tell each other what their schedules were, where they were going to be, what leads they were going to check, and stay out of each other's way.

She stood. "Well, I'm bushed. I have a few leads to check out in the morning," which was a lie, "so why don't we make contact tomorrow afternoon. You can call me here." That way she didn't have to see him and have temptation, ludicrous as it was, thrown in her face again. She grabbed her purse and walked around her desk toward the door, trying to keep some distance between them. "Come on, Beau."

Mick stood lazily and moved to open the door. "I'll walk you to your car."

She didn't want him to walk her to her car, or anywhere else for that matter. Arm's length—no, the length of a ten-foot pole was where she needed to keep him, at least until her mind could convince her body that she wasn't really attracted to him. "Ah, no thanks. I have to lock up. You go ahead."

He smiled. "I'll help."

Five minutes later they were at her car. B.J. hurriedly opened the driver's door and glanced over her shoulder at Mick while Beaujolais jumped into the car and settled himself onto the passenger seat. "Well, thanks for dinner. Good night."

Mick caught B.J.'s arm and pulled her back. He was crossing the line, letting his emotions overrule his usual good sense, but for the moment he didn't care. All he wanted was to feel her body pressed against his, taste the sweetness of her lips. It was something he'd been wanting to do since the first moment he'd walked into her office, and though that wasn't all that long ago, a matter of hours really, he wasn't a patient man. He was tired of denying his attraction to her.

Before B.J. realized what was happening, she was caught in the circle of his arms and unbearably conscious of exactly where his body was touching hers. She heard a faint voice from the back of her mind scream at her to break away from him, to wrench herself free of his embrace. Instead, she remained still, acutely aware of the pulsing knot that had begun to form in her stomach, the suddenly crashing beat of her heart, and the quivering that had attacked her knees.

His body, all rippling muscles and rock-hard lines, seemed to fit against hers perfectly, line for line, curve for curve, as if each had been shaped to meld with the other.

Tricks of the Trade

She felt her blood surge and race madly from her fingertips to her toes, while the scent of him surrounded and intoxicated her.

She waited, knowing she should pull away from him, sensing on the thin thread of rationality that had not yet deserted her, that she was in more trouble, more danger, than she'd ever encountered before in her life.

"I've wanted to kiss you since the first moment I walked into your office," Mick said.

His hands slipped to her waist, crushing her against him. B.J. knew that in spite of all her silent denials, she was exactly where she'd wanted to be all evening.

She could feel his uneven breathing caress the curve of her cheek. The touch of his hand on her back sent a warm shiver racing up her spine, and, as her hands slid up the length of his arms, she found the feel of hard muscle to be an unexpected intoxicant.

The scent of the day clung to him, a blend of wintry crispness and Mardi Gras wickedness that was uniquely New Orleans. But beneath that she detected a scent that was distinctly him, a mixture of man and seduction that was so heady to B.J. that reality, all her hesitations and worries, disappeared as swiftly as if carried away by a wind.

Cocking his head to one side, Mick gently pressed his lips to the side of B.J.'s neck, and a quiet gasp slipped from her lips as a wave of delicious shivers raced through her body. A trembling weakness followed, moving swiftly through her to rob her of all will and strength.

As if intending to torment her, Mick continued to nuzzle the flesh at the curve of her neck with his lips, nipping softly, sliding his tongue upward along the thin vein that showed itself, ever so slightly, from the hollow of her collarbone to the base of her jaw. Then he worked his way back down, pressing his lips into the hollow of her throat. That small basin of flesh was an area of passionate sensitivity no man had ever explored before, and one B.J. had not known existed.

"No," she whispered softly. But whether it was an entreaty for him to stop the sweet torture he seemed determined to inflict upon her, or a plea for him to continue, even she wasn't sure.

With tormenting slowness his lips moved upward again, along her neck, along the curve of her jaw, until his mouth unerringly sought and found hers.

His kiss was hesitant at first, but when she didn't resist him, his mouth became hard and hot on hers, igniting a series of explosions deep inside of her. Blood pounded in B.J.'s brain, her heart thudded madly against her breast, and her knees trembled violently. Her hands slid over his shoulders and she clung to him, shocked at her own response to the touch of his lips and never wanting the sensation to end.

Flesh melded to flesh in a kiss that was smoldering heat and tantalizing persuasion. The caress of his tongue against hers was like a daring challenge, and one she sought to meet, her own tongue, her hands, her body, yearning to stoke the fires that had gripped them both. Her soul was aflame with the need of him, her senses reeling, any control as if short-circuited or merely forgotten about.

Nothing in her life had prepared her for Mick Gentry,

Tricks of the Trade

or the feelings, the needs and yearnings his kiss was bringing forth within her.

A low and very menacing growl suddenly sounded behind them.

Jerked back to reality by the threatening sound, B.J. took a staggering step back toward the car as Mick, still holding her with one hand, spun around.

"Get out of here," Mick ordered, his voice just as low and menacing as the growl of the mangy-looking German shepherd who was staring past them and into the car at Beaujolais.

When the dog merely growled again, bared his teeth, and didn't move, Mick's free hand went to rest on the butt of his gun, and he stamped his foot. "Go," he yelled at the same time.

The dog bolted toward the corner.

Mick turned back to B.J., but as he looked into her eyes, both knew the moment of passion had passed, and both knew the other regretted that it had ever happened.

B.J. looked in her bathroom mirror and groaned. She had spent a very long night trying to sleep, but thoughts of Mick Gentry kept getting in the way. Now she looked as tired as she felt. "Whoever said romance was good for the soul was crazy," she mumbled, grabbing for her toothpaste.

Or at least whoever said it didn't take into consideration what it did to the psyche. She looked back at her image and mentally ticked off what she'd have to do to cover the damage of a sleepless night. Today was not a day she could get away with wearing no makeup, that was for sure.

Half an hour later, dressed in turquoise slacks, a matching blazer, and a white silk blouse, B.J. was ready to go. She'd taken great care in applying her makeup—foundation, mascara, a touch of shadow, and lipstick—so there was almost no visible trace of her restless night. Unless one looked too close.

She drained the last of the coffee from her cup and left for the office. A brushed and beribboned Beaujolais pranced daintily at her heels.

"I'm glad you're so bouncy this morning," she said as the tiny dog jumped into the car ahead of her. "How about lending me some of your energy?" She straightened the blue ribbon attached to his collar.

Beaujolais yipped, and B.J. smiled. "Right."

It only took ten minutes to get to her office. As she rounded the corner of the building after parking her car, B.J. stopped dead in her tracks. "Oh, great," she muttered.

Mick Gentry, all six foot two inches of hard muscle and arrogance, stood lazily against the entrance of the building, one booted foot propped up against the wall, his hat pushed low, and his chin resting on his chest, like a great cat dozing. But B.J. knew now that Mick Gentry was anything but a lazy, dozing cat. And if she hadn't already been convinced of that, she would have been when he looked up and she saw the grim line of determination that was his mouth. "More like an extremely cunning wolf in sheep's clothing," she grumbled to herself.

"Little piggy, little piggy, let me in," she mumbled

mockingly, "or I'll huff and I'll puff and I'll blow your house down." She had a quick flash of the elegant brick Pontalba building in which her office was located, suddenly crumbling to the ground.

Beaujolais pranced ahead of her and greeted Mick happily, wagging his tail and propping his front feet on Mick's leg.

B.J. glared down at her dog. "Judas," she whispered. She looked at Mick and forced a smile to her lips. "What are you doing here so early?"

"We're working together. Or did you forget?"

"I thought we agreed that you were going to call me this afternoon." She brushed past him and headed for the stairs, noticing on her way, and with a glimmer of satisfaction, that he looked as if he hadn't gotten any more sleep than she had.

"That's not my idea of working together," Mick said, following her.

Great, great, great. She'd thought, hoped, that although she'd given in and agreed to work with him, they'd actually go their separate ways and only confer once in a while on what they'd come up with.

Beaujolais started dancing about and yipping excitedly the moment they reached the second floor landing. It should have been a warning, but B.J. was too absorbed in trying to figure out how she was going to get out of spending the entire day with Mick Gentry to give much thought to the dog's strange behavior.

She pushed open the door to her office and gasped. "Good grief, what is this?" She stared at the sea of dogs that filled the reception room.

"Welcome to doggyland," Alice quipped from behind her desk, shooing a fluffy bit of whiteness away from her legs.

"Oh, no." B.J. groaned. She flashed a glance over her shoulder at Mick. The amusement she saw in his eyes didn't reassure her. Scooping Beaujolais up and into her arms before he could challenge any of the other dogs in the room, since they had invaded his territory, she weaved her way through the playing, snarling, sleeping, preening mass of canine bodies.

Cries of "I've found your dog" assaulted her from all directions as the people attached to the other ends of the leashes saw her and assumed correctly that she was B.J. Poydras.

"Come into my office," B.J. snapped at Alice, then dived for her door.

"Him too?" Alice said, looking at Mick.

She wanted to say no. "Yes."

B.J. whirled around the minute the door closed. "What in heaven's name happened? Where did all those dogs come from? And, though I have the horrible feeling I know the answer, why are they here?"

Mick, trying to stifle the grin that was desperately tugging at the corners of his mouth, slipped into one of the chairs facing her desk while Alice cocked a hip, slammed a hand onto it, and threw B.J. a mocking glare. "And just which question do you want answered first?"

"Alice," B.J. snapped.

"Okay, okay." She was barely able to keep the laughter from her voice. "It seems that Mrs. Charbonneau put an ad, complete with a reward offering, in last night's paper." She handed it to B.J., who stared at the words within the red circle Alice had drawn on the paper.

"Twenty-five-thousand dollars?" she said with a gasp. "But why did she hire me if she was going to do this?"

"Reward for what?" Mick mused, leaning forward in his chair. He didn't know what was going on, but he had an idea that whatever it was, it was going to be good.

The smile she saw on his face irked her beyond reason, and the spark of humor that danced in his eyes was more than she could tolerate.

B.J. slammed the paper down on her desk, the article face down. "Nothing."

SIX

"I think I'll leave you alone to explain," Alice said, throwing B.J. a rather sheepish smile and backing toward the door.

Mortified at the prospect of having to admit the truth to Mick, furious with herself for feeling that way and, unreasonably, at Alice for not getting rid of the dogs before she and Mick arrived, B.J.'s gaze darted away from Mick to shoot Alice a look that was intended to be lethal. "Thank you," she said, her tone as deadly as the look flashing in her eyes.

"No problem, boss." Alice had regained a bit of her bravado. "Oh, and there's a pot of fresh coffee over there on the counter."

The door shut, and Beaujolais wiggled out of B.J.'s arms, hit the floor with a thud, and trotted to the door. He sniffed at its base and growled softly.

"It's okay, Beau," B.J. said, ignoring Mick and moving around her desk to sit down.

Tricks of the Trade

Mick poured them each a cup of coffee, set one down on the desk before her, then resettled himself in the chair. "Okay, what's the reward for?"

This isn't really happening, B.J. told herself, turning her back to him and staring through the window. But then, why not? Hadn't she lived with Murphy's Law most of her life?

Five years earlier she'd fallen in love with an engineer. Two months before they were to be married, he took off with B.J.'s best friend from college. Then there was the lawyer whose wealthy mother threatened to cut him off if he married a P.I.—naturally he dropped B.J. like a ton of rotten crawfish. She'd followed up that fiasco by becoming involved with a local politician who, at election time, decided he had a better chance at the fast track to Washington by having a blue-blooded debutante who wanted nothing more than to be at his side as his wife and the mother of his children.

Then there were B.J.'s parents. Dr. Etienne Jay Poydras thought his eldest daughter's foray into the world of private investigations was "cute," and of course merely a diversion until she found Mr. Right, while her society-minded mother most times refused to speak to her, saying they would converse when she agreed to stop "scandalizing" the entire family and came to her senses.

"B.J.?" Mick said, tired of waiting for a response and breaking into her thoughts.

She swiveled toward him, knowing exactly what Marie Antoinette must have felt like when she'd placed her neck on the chopping block. The feeling didn't sit well. B.J. stared at Mick defiantly, telling herself that even if her waiting room had come to resemble a doggie grooming parlor, nothing had really changed. She still didn't have to tell him anything if she didn't want to.

She was just about to conjure up another fib when, before she could stop him, Mick grabbed the folded newspaper from her desk.

His gaze went straight to the red circle Alice had drawn around the ad. "Twenty-five-thousand-dollar reward for information leading to the return of miniature white poodle, show cut, answering to the name ChiChi," he read aloud. "Contact B.J. Poydras Investigations, Vieux Carré. 555-5683." He set the paper down and looked up at her.

She expected him to laugh. To ridicule her. To jeer her as an investigator. Instead, fury blazed from narrowed eyes, settled into the hard line of his jaw, and pulsed from the thin vein on the side of his neck that had abruptly become all too prominent.

"Why'd you lie to me?" His blue eyes, suddenly as dark as night and full of bitterness and resentment, stared into hers as he waited for her answer.

"I didn't," she snapped automatically. "I mean, not really. You assumed and I . . ." The words "let you" died before being muttered. Humiliation burned B.J.'s cheeks. She felt herself withering under his intense scrutiny.

"You lied," Mick said again, the tone of his voice like the lash of a whip to her senses.

B.J. opened her mouth to respond but was stalled as he pushed abruptly to his feet. The smoldering rage she sensed emanating from him seemed to steal the air from the room.

"Mick, I—"

"Never mind," he said, cutting her off.

Panic at the fact that he was leaving and the unforeseen realization that she didn't want him to go, filled B.J. For the past two days she'd been trying to find a way to get rid of him, and now, the saints have mercy on her soul, she didn't want him to go. "Mick, really I didn't mean to . . . Well, I mean, I did, but . . ."

He stared down at her. A frown dug into his forehead, dragging his brows together. Then it disappeared, and his eyes grew even colder, his features seeming to harden to stone right before her eyes.

"You lied to me."

"Well, yes, ah, technically," she stammered, "but . . ."

"It doesn't matter."

The words were full of bitterness and rigidly curt, but the expression in his eyes was inscrutable. Was it intense fury that clouded his eyes or total apathy? B.J. wasn't sure which it was, but shuddered at the realization she desperately wanted it to be neither.

Before she could think of something to say, he spun on his heel and stalked to the door. A series of yipping barks erupted when he opened it, but all B.J. was aware of was his retreating back as he stalked a path through the little dogs. She heard the outer door slam shut.

"What happened?" Alice said, hurrying into B.J.'s office and closing the door behind her.

B.J. was so shaken by a turmoil of emotions—some

yearning, some anger, but not the least of which was intense humiliation—that she could hardly speak. Jumping up, she moved to the window and stared down into the square.

"B.J.," Alice said again, "what happened?"

"I think you just saw what happened," she said, continuing to stare past the window. "U.S. marshals obviously don't work with pet detectives."

"You're not a pet detective," Alice said.

B.J. swung around. "Oh? And how many other private investigators do you know whose reception room looks like the local animal shelter?"

"Mrs. Charbonneau's case is a legitimate one," Alice argued, "and a profitable one."

"Keep saying that, Alice," B.J. grumbled, slumping back into her chair. "It makes me feel better."

Beaujolais jumped onto B.J.'s lap. She looked down at him and smiled. "You're the one to blame for this whole mess, you know." She tweaked the dog's ear. "If I didn't know that I'd be just as upset about losing you as Mrs. Charbonneau is at losing ChiChi, I never would have taken this case."

"The money doesn't hurt either," Alice said.

B.J. looked up. "No, it doesn't."

"So, what do I do about them?" Alice jabbed a thumb toward the reception room.

B.J. sighed. "Do any of them even come close to resembling ChiChi?"

"Three. But only slightly."

"I guess I should at least check them out."

"And the others?"

B.J. shrugged. If truth be told she didn't care about the others, or even the three remote possibilities, because at the moment she didn't even care about the case. She wanted to know where a certain U.S. marshal had gone, and if there was even the slightest possibility he'd ever talk to her again. "Refer them to the animal shelter, I guess."

Mick knew what was in every shop adjacent to Jackson Square because in the past hour he'd paced in front of each of them more times than he wanted to count.

He was frustrated and furious and in the mood to take someone's head off. The only reason he'd wanted to work with B.J. was to make things easier and wrap up his case faster. He knew Townsend was connected to Charbonneau somehow but all of his own inquiries had run into a dead end. Townsend's parents were dead. He had an aunt and uncle, but they were in their nineties and in a rest home. His only other known relative, a cousin and accomplice in the robbery, had died in a car accident a few months after Townsend was sent to prison. And the trail that had led Mick to New Orleans had gone ice cold.

He'd believed that since Mrs. Charbonneau had hired a private investigator, the only smart thing to do was find out what the P.I. had already turned up. It was just his bad luck that Charbonneau's P.I. was a woman. Worse, that she was an attractive woman, and his body had obviously taken notice, in spite of his determined objections. And he needed her, in more ways than one. B.J. knew the ins and outs of the city, she had local contacts, and she had access to Mrs. Charbonneau—all things Mick didn't have.

But she'd lied to him, dammit, and that was something he didn't tolerate. Disappointment pierced him. Sherry had lied to him, told him everything was still all right. Promised they'd work things out. Swore she still loved him. They had all been lies, and she'd known it even when she was saying them. But like a fool, he'd believed her.

Mick walked past the ice cream parlor again, nearly running over a man draped in cameras and kids on his way out. Not even noticing, Mick kept pacing. He'd sworn the day Sherry left that if he ever caught a woman lying to him, he'd never trust that person again. Never believe another word she said, or have anything to do with her after that if he could help it.

But he was having a hard time making himself walk away from B.J. And he had the most awful feeling that it wasn't just the case that was compelling him to stick around.

A soft curse rumbled up from his throat. He didn't need her cooperation to solve his case. Mick flexed his fingers, then curled them into fists. He had tracked Townsend this far without her help, he could go the rest of the way. The problem was, he didn't want to, and that was a problem he'd never encountered before. For the past four years he'd been a loner, preferring it that way, shunning his boss's every suggestion of taking on a partner or helping to train a rookie. He worked alone, depended on no one but himself. So why in blazes was he so preoccupied with B.J. Poydras? Why didn't he just leave and let her go chase down the mutt she was hired to find?

Mick grumbled under his breath, drawing a cautious glance from an elderly passerby. He forced himself to smile, but rather than looking reassured, the woman averted her gaze nervously and hurried away.

Mick continued to pace. The best thing he could do was walk away, right now. Put his nose to the grindstone where it belonged, solve his case, apprehend Townsend and, as his father used to say, get the hell out of Dodge.

But he wasn't going to do that, and he didn't have the faintest idea why.

Stepping away from the building, he walked to the fence that surrounded the square and stared up at the window of B.J.'s office.

He cared about her. The acknowledgment struck him between the eyes as soundly as if someone had shot him.

B.J. watched the last of the three possibilities leave her office. None of the dogs had answered to the name ChiChi, but in the end it hadn't mattered. The first had been too old, the second too young, and the third the wrong sex. Drooping back against her chair she sighed, but whether from relief at the fact that the interviews were over, or in defeat that Mick Gentry was gone and most likely was not coming back, she wasn't sure.

B.J. picked up the Charbonneau case folder that sat on her desk, then slapped it down and rose. She began to pace her office and tried to force herself to concentrate on finding Mrs. Charbonneau's dog. But she was out of ideas. There was nowhere else to look. Theodore Charbonneau was lying in the morgue, supposedly, and not one animal shelter, adoption agency, or lost and found ad had come up with a dog that matched ChiChi's description. For the moment, B.J. didn't really care. She paused and looked through the window again, then realized she was scanning the square in the hopes of seeing Mick Gentry. "Oh, wonderful," she snapped at herself. "What do you think, that he's out there pining away after you? Wishing he hadn't left?"

Beaujolais, obviously thinking she was talking to him, yipped.

"Oh, be quiet, you little traitor," B.J. said. Anger burned in B.J.'s breast. She didn't care about Mick Gentry. He was an arrogant, self-righteous, bull-headed know-it-all, and she didn't care about him one iota. She should be glad he was gone. Wasn't that what she'd been wishing for? So who needed him? She had a case to solve, and it had nothing to do with his.

Turning back to her desk, she was just about to call it a morning and go find a place to eat lunch and wallow in self-pity when the intercom sounded. B.J. ignored it, and it buzzed again. She grabbed the receiver of her phone. "What?"

Alice chuckled. "I think this call will make you feel better."

Hope flashed through her. B.J. immediately tried to squash it, but couldn't help asking, "Is it . . . ?"

"No, but you'll feel better anyway."

Maybe if someone was calling to tell her she'd won a million-dollar lottery, she'd feel better. She smashed down the button whose light was blinking. "This is B.J. Poydras," she said, her tone curt, cold, and hard, relaying to the caller, she hoped, that she was in no mood to chitchat.

"B.J., *ma douce*, oooh, my, my, my, you don't sound too happy, *cherie*."

She smiled. Harley D'Cambre was a good contact, always there with information, sometimes even before she knew she needed it. "Well I don't feel happy today, Harley, so make me feel better. What've you got for me?"

"Well, *cherie*, I hear yo' been looking 'bout for info on some rich dude name o' Theodore Charbonneau."

"Kind of. What's up?"

"Him havin' a mistress interest yo' any, *cherie*?"

B.J. sat up, suddenly very interested. "Yes. Do you have a name for me?"

"Ah, c'mon, *cherie*. Do catfish swim?"

"Harley."

"*Mais* sho', *mais* sho', *ma petite*." He laughed, the sound reminding B.J. of a rattling skeleton. "Yo' send ol' Harley a lil' somethin' for the info, *cherie*?"

"Don't I always?"

"Yeah, yo' good to me, *ma jolie*. Listen, yor ol' rich boy, Charbonneau, he been makin' time with a stripper by the name of Evie Strindel. Works down at Dixie's on Bourbon, and she ain't no innocent, if yo' know what I mean, *cherie*."

"I know. Thanks, Harley." B.J. hung up. *Douce* and *jolie*, sweet and pretty: Harley might think so, but then she paid him. Mick Gentry would probably scoff.

B.J. didn't know exactly what she had to gain by going

down to the strip and talking to Charbonneau's mistress, but it couldn't hurt. And maybe, just maybe if she was really lucky, the woman had ChiChi.

Grabbing her bag, she started for the door, then stopped and walked back to her desk. Opening its bottom drawer she pulled out the small derringer she only carried when she thought she might be going somewhere a "tad" unsafe. She had no idea what she was getting into or with whom. Slipping the gun into her purse, B.J. walked into the reception area. "Alice, I'm going down to a club on Bourbon. Would you mind taking Beaujolais out for a walk in the square later? And if I'm late, take him back to my place?"

"No problem. How long do you think you'll be?"

"Only a couple of hours, I hope."

"And if the marshal calls?"

B.J. shrugged. "He won't."

B.J. pushed open the door to the street and stepped out onto the banquette.

Mick saw her immediately and pushed away from the wall where he'd been standing.

Out of the corner of her eye B.J. caught a blur of blue. Turning, she felt her heart beat faster at recognizing him, then told herself her reaction was only because he'd startled her by being there. She smiled stiffly as he neared.

"Got a lead?" The question came out a little more terse than Mick had intended, but his anger wasn't likely to go away too soon.

"I thought you didn't want to . . ."

"Forget that. I don't give a damn how you're working the Charbonneau case, it still has itself tangled up in mine. Now, where to?"

B.J. glared up at him. "Look, Marshal, if you think you can snap my head off one minute, then expect me to work with you the next, you're—"

"Just don't lie to me again," he said tightly, "and we'll get along fine."

B.J. felt her temper rising when a slow, easy grin pulled the corners of his mouth upward, and her heart nearly melted. "Now, like I said before, where are we going?"

"Well first, I'm going to get some lunch." The way he seemed itching to get moving, she prayed sitting down to lunch would be too much to ask and he'd go stomping off on his own. "I'm starving."

"Great. So am I. Didn't have much breakfast."

B.J. sighed. So much for that tactic. "But no talking business," she said, trying again.

"Fine. We'll talk about what you did before you became a P.I."

"And you?" she urged.

Settling his Stetson back on his head, Mick grinned down at her. "My story can be summed up in just a couple of sentences, and it's boring. I think I'd like yours better."

She felt her heart give a little lurch as their gazes met. Blue melded with blue for just a split second before she forced herself to look away. She'd been right. This man was extremely dangerous, and it had nothing to do with the fact that he carried a gun beneath his jacket.

B.J. finished off the last of her sandwich and sat back, the umbrella overhead shading her from the sun. "So, now you know all about me," she said, still wondering what in the world had prompted her to answer all of his personal questions, something she'd never in her life done for any of the other men she'd dated—but then most of them had been locals and knew her life story anyway. "But I don't know anything more about you than I did an hour ago. You're a U.S. marshal and you have a ranch in Nevada."

"Just outside of Reno," he said, and smiled.

"Is that where you lived when you were married?"

He took several bills from his wallet, tossed them onto the table where the check lay, and stood. "So, where are we off to?" he asked, ignoring her question.

B.J. frowned. *He'd changed the subject—my question must have made him touchy.* The moment the thought entered her brain she mentally cringed. What did she care if he was touchy about the subject of his past, especially about his marriage? He was an annoyance she evidently had to put up with for the moment, that was all. She wasn't interested in him. No way. Not in the least. Never.

And you're not interested in breathing anymore either, a little voice at the back of her mind teased.

She rejected it and looked at Mick. "We're going to Bourbon Street. Ready?"

"Yeah. I'll drive."

B.J. bristled at what she considered his imperious tone. "We can take my car."

"Mine's closer," Mick said.

She looked up at him. "How do you know?"

He smiled again. "I know." Stopping at the curb, he motioned toward the sedan that was parked there, then opened the door for her.

B.J. slid onto the passenger seat, not certain she liked the arrangement, but not wanting to make a scene about it.

Mick walked around the car and climbed into the driver's seat.

B.J. glanced at him out of the corner of her eye. Why did they make cars so small and cowboys so big?

It should have taken less than five minutes to drive to Bourbon Street, park, and enter Dixie's Club. Instead, there was construction on St. Louis and Chartres, and they got caught in the gridlock of cars waiting to cross the intersection.

B.J. inhaled deeply in an effort to calm her suddenly racing pulse. The scent of his cologne overwhelmed her, and to her horror her body reacted as if just given an aphrodisiac. She felt her hands tremble, her heart thud, and . . . oh, she didn't even want to acknowledge the aching heat that seemed to have invaded every cell in her body.

She eyed the door handle and wondered if she dare jump out of the car.

"About time," Mick said with irony.

B.J. jumped, startled, and looked at him just as the car started to move forward.

Two minutes later they walked into Dixie's Social Club.

"I'll handle this," she whispered as they approached the bar.

Mick shrugged. "Fine by me."

B.J. glanced at the small name tag on the bartender's shirtfront, then gave him a smile. "Ben, we're looking for Evie Strindel."

The bartender, a burly man with a handlebar mustache and a well-shined bald pate, looked them up and down. "So who are you?"

"A friend."

"Yeah," he said with a snarl, "and I'm James Bond."

"He should look so good," B.J. cooed.

The man instantly preened.

"Oh brother," Mick said under his breath.

B.J. slapped him with a cool glare. She turned back to the bartender. "My name is B.J. Poydras. I'm a private investigator, and I have reason to believe Evie might be in trouble. Maybe even in danger."

"Evie doesn't work here anymore," Ben said.

"She quit?" B.J. said, surprised.

He shook his head. "Not really. We just ain't heard from her in awhile, so we figured she ain't coming back." He shrugged. "But you never know with these girls."

"How long has it been?"

He shrugged again. "I don't know, but she was pretty close with Lola, if you want to ask her. She's backstage."

"Thanks," B.J. said, "I'll do that."

"But not him," Ben said, nodding at Mick. "No guys allowed backstage."

She felt Mick stiffen, got a little rush of satisfaction at the thought of making him wait at the bar for her, then

Tricks of the Trade

reconsidered. Sometimes a woman would open up for a handsome man when she wouldn't for another woman. B.J. smiled. "Oh, but I can't leave him out here," she pleaded softly. She dropped her voice to just above a whisper. "See, he's my brother and he's mentally . . ." She looked around, as if embarrassed. "Well, he's slow, you know? Real slow, and I just can't leave him alone." She sighed. "He gets in fights when I leave him alone."

Ben eyed Mick, who decided right then and there that when they got back outside he was going to strangle B.J. But for the moment, having been given no choice, he tried to look simple.

"I don't know," Ben said. "It's against the rules."

Mick hurriedly hooked a finger into the corner of his mouth and attempted to give the impression he was ready to start crying. "He's lookin' at me funny, B.," he whined.

"It's okay, Mickey," B.J. said, patting his arm. She turned back to the bartender. "Please, Ben. He won't be any trouble if he stays with me. I promise."

Ben nodded. "Okay. But keep an eye on him."

They walked toward the curtained-off backstage door.

"Been just aching to do something like that, haven't you?" Mick whispered.

"Shhh." B.J. struggled not to laugh. "Someone will hear."

"That's going to be the least of your worries later."

"Is that a threat?" she teased. B.J. knew she was playing with fire, but somehow couldn't stop herself.

"Yes, and if I get caught, I'll just plead diminished capacity due to inhuman harassment."

She pushed aside the curtain and came face to face

with a redhead who towered over her by at least a foot. B.J. looked up, trying to ignore the fact that the woman's breasts, each covered only by a tiny piece of sequined material, were almost in her face. Stretching to try to give herself a little more height, and a little distance from those protruding mounds of flesh, B.J. smiled. "I'm looking for Lola."

"And who's he looking for?" the woman purred, settling her heavily mascaraed green eyes on Mick.

"Lola," B.J. said.

The woman's brows lifted in interest, her ruby red, highly glossed lips twitched into a smile, and as she put her hands on her hips her breasts thrust forward another inch, almost colliding with B.J.'s nose. "Ummm, well then, you've found her."

"You're Lola?" B.J. asked, taking a step back and running into Mick.

"In the flesh," the woman purred, still directing both her gaze and comments toward Mick. "So, what can I do for you, handsome?"

B.J. glanced over her shoulder and saw him smiling at the stripper. Jealousy, hot, burning, and totally unexpected, flashed through her. She stiffened against it and turned back to Lola, harboring a pretty good idea what the stripper would like to do for Mick.

"We need to know where Evie Strindel is," B.J. said.

"Come on and have a drink with me, handsome, and we'll discuss it." She turned and began to walk away, her rear end swinging like a pendulum.

B.J. fumed. If there was one thing she didn't like, it was being ignored. "Ms. . . . ah, Lola, I . . ."

Tricks of the Trade

Mick touched her shoulder. "I think that's the manager of the place over there," he said, pointing toward a wiry-looking man standing across the room near the stage. "Why don't you go see what he knows, and I'll deal with Lola."

"I'll bet you will," B.J. said, jerking her shoulder away from his hand and marching across the stage.

SEVEN

"We're not hiring."

B.J. looked at the man Mick had directed her to, presumably the bar's manager, her brows rising just a bit at his presumption that she was looking for a job. "I'm not applying," she said testily.

A stub of cigar that seemed permanently settled into the right corner of his mouth suddenly shifted position to the left side. The man reminded her of someone out of a 1970s movie about the Mafia, his hair styled into a pompadour, complete with sideburns to his jawline, silk shirt open to his waist, giving full view of a very hairy chest, a tangle of gold necklaces, a stomach well on its way to being a paunch, and a huge gold pinky ring shaped like a lion's head with a ruby in its mouth.

He looked up from the clipboard he was holding and gave her a quick once-over. "That's good, honey, 'cause you haven't got enough curves."

B.J. was determined to control her temper, if for no

Tricks of the Trade

other reason than she needed answers from him, *if* he was the manager. Besides, she didn't feel like being arrested for assault and battery, or having a mob contract put out on her life. "Are you the manager of this place?"

"Yeah, so?"

She flipped open the wallet with her ID card and held it out toward him.

He glanced at her ID. "Wow," he said with a sneer, "I'm impressed."

"I thought you would be," B.J. said, just as sarcastically. "I'm trying to locate Evie Strindel. I understand she worked here."

"She hasn't been in for awhile."

"How long?"

He shrugged and scribbled something onto his clipboard. "I don't know exactly. Ask Lola."

"I tried that. Do you have an address on her?"

"Probably."

"Can I have it?"

He looked up, a deep frown turning his face ugly. "Evie in trouble?"

"Maybe more than she can handle," B.J. said, not even certain if she was lying or telling the truth. "Maybe less if I can find her before the cops do," she added for good measure.

He turned and walked toward a door set in the far wall and half obscured by shadow. "Come on," he called over his shoulder.

B.J. hastened to follow him into a cluttered little office where he immediately started sifting through a mound of papers piled on a desk in the center of the room.

"Evie's a good kid," he muttered. "I'd hate to see her get herself in trouble." He pulled out another clipboard and, after jerking off one piece of paper after another, held one out to B.J. "Here. This is all I got on her."

B.J. looked at the employment form, noting the address. Esplanade. That had been an elite address once, but that was a long time ago. "Thanks," she said, and turned to go.

"If you see her, tell Evie she can come back to work."

B.J. looked back, surprised. She wouldn't have expected generosity from him. But maybe he and Evie had more going on between them than employer and employee. That made her stop and wonder further. If there was something between Evie and this guy, could it have anything to do with Theodore Charbonneau's death . . . or disappearance?

Back in the dimly lit bar, she saw that Mick was waiting for her at the door to the street.

"Get an address?" he asked as she neared.

"Yes," she said, feeling a surge of satisfaction.

"Good. I got a name." He smiled at her perplexed look.

"A name?"

He nodded. "Yeah, and it wasn't Theodore Charbonneau."

B.J. stopped as the sun hit her eyes. She blinked and looked at Mick. "Wait a minute. You mean Evie was seeing someone besides Charbonneau?"

He shrugged. "I don't know, but Lola swears that Evie's boyfriend was named Carter."

"Carter?" B.J. repeated.

"Yeah. Her description of him sounded like your guy, though. Short, balding, lots of money."

Ten minutes later, after following B.J.'s directions, Mick pulled his rental car up in front of the address the manager had given B.J. It was a large old Victorian house, once probably one of the most opulent in the city. Now it was merely old, faded, and in desperate need of renovation. It had also been cut up into apartments, as had most of the other buildings on the block.

Mick started to open his car door.

"Why don't you wait here?" B.J. said.

"Wait here?" He looked at her suspiciously. "Why?"

She smiled. "Because Evie might be more willing to talk than bolt if it's a woman at her door."

Mick thought that over for a few seconds, then nodded, though B.J. could see from the look in his eyes that he didn't like the idea of being left behind.

She climbed from the car and walked up the pathway to the house. It was an old multi-gabled design, with fancy woodwork, arched windows, and intricately carved balustrades. But if someone didn't do something to save it soon, it would most likely be beyond help. She sighed. There were too many buildings like this in New Orleans, elegant old ladies with a hundred stories to tell, a wealth of history within their walls, and all falling into ruin.

B.J. rang the buzzer for Evie Strindel's apartment, but got no response. After another try, with still no answer, she glanced over her shoulder at Mick and rang for the manager.

The voice that responded sounded like it had endured

one too many cigarettes. "We ain't got no rooms for rent."

"I'm looking for Evie Strindel," B.J. said quickly.

The door immediately buzzed open. B.J. entered, and the same froggy voice croaked, "Down here."

B.J. passed a staircase and proceeded down the hall to where a woman who looked a lot like an eighty-year-old hooker stood waiting.

"Evie didn't answer her buzz, so I thought you might know where she is," B.J. said.

"I wish I did," the woman said. "She left without paying last month's rent."

"I have reason to believe she might be in trouble." B.J. hoped she sounded worried enough to get the woman to cooperate. "Do you think you might let me look in her apartment? See if I can figure out where she might have gone?"

"Sure honey, then you can tell me so I can get my rent money."

The woman tramped up the stairs, feather-covered bedroom slippers slapping at her heels as she walked. She stopped at a door just off the landing, and opened it with a key that hung from a chain around her neck. "Here you go," the landlady said, waving B.J. into the room.

B.J. entered and stopped dead in the center of a room filled with very expensive furniture. She turned back to the landlady, who was still standing in the doorway. "Is this furniture hers?"

The woman looked around and let out her version of a wolf whistle. "Not anymore it ain't," she said. "I'm confiscating it in lieu of that back rent she owes me."

Tricks of the Trade

In B.J.'s opinion, Evie was getting the short end of the deal. Why would a woman who could afford furniture like this live in a dump on Esplanade? Unless this was just a front and she had a nicer place elsewhere. She turned back to the landlady. "Did Evie really live here? I mean, did you see her here every day?"

"Hey, I ain't nosey, you know? My tenants' business is their own business." The woman glared at B.J.

"I'm sorry, I didn't mean that, I just want to make certain this was her main place of residence, that's all."

The woman eyed her suspiciously, then nodded. "Yeah, she lived here. This apartment's right above mine, used to hear her up here all the time with her men friends."

"Men friends?" B.J. echoed.

"Yeah. Woman had more men flitting about her than honey has bees."

"Not just one in particular?" B.J. persisted.

The woman shrugged. "Not that I saw."

Five minutes later, after going through the nearly empty closets and dresser drawers, B.J. knew that Evie had definitely deserted the place. She walked back into the living room and handed the landlady her card. "If you hear from her, give me a call, would you?"

"Any reward?" The woman's eager eyes darted from the card to B.J. and back again.

"Maybe," B.J. said, figuring, without that incentive the woman wouldn't call even if Evie showed up that night accompanied by the Army/Navy football teams.

"I want to stop by the police station and check on a few things," Mick said when B.J. climbed back into the car and told him Evie had skipped out.

"Okay. Drop me at my office," B.J. said.

"After."

She glared at him. Did the man purposely try to rile her, or did it just come naturally to him? She sat back, arms crossed over her chest, and stared out the window as they drove toward the French Quarter. The station wasn't that far from her office. She'd just walk. And never consent to go anywhere with Mick Gentry in his car again.

"The coroner should have a few test results in by now."

"Probably," B.J. said.

"You're still convinced it's Charbonneau in the morgue?"

"I have no proof it's not," B.J. said.

"And you have only circumstantial evidence that it is."

B.J. shrugged. "That's enough. Anyway, I don't care."

"Oh yeah, I forgot, you're only interested in the dog." Mick looked at her questioningly. As long as he kept their conversation on business he was okay. Why he was getting the hots every five minutes for a woman who seemed to have the extraordinary ability to push him straight from calm to furious in nothing flat, was beyond his understanding.

"Mrs. Charbonneau is satisfied that the dead man is her husband," B.J. said hotly. "The coroner is satisfied that the dead man is Charbonneau, and so are the police,

Tricks of the Trade

and everyone but you is satisfied that his death was an accident, so yes," she said snippily, "I am only interested in finding the dog. There's nothing more to find."

"You're wrong," Mick said. "Townsend used Charbonneau's credit card in San Francisco to buy a ring, we have proof of that, and Townsend followed Charbonneau here to New Orleans, then disappeared."

"Maybe he just left town."

"And maybe I'm President of the United States," Mick said.

"Heaven save us from that." She went on before he could respond. "He's a crook, right? On the run, right? Maybe he pulled off a job we don't know about and figured he'd better leave town. Or maybe he went somewhere else to pull a job."

"If he pulled off a job, I'd have heard about it," Mick said. "If he left, why'd he come here in the first place?"

"Maybe he was just giving you a trail to follow, maybe he was just trying to lose you, maybe he was just traveling aimlessly. I don't know," B.J. said, getting more frustrated and irritated by the moment.

"Yeah, maybe," Mick said. He waited a few seconds before making another comment. "I think that's Carl Townsend in the morgue and Charbonneau killed him, then took off."

"Why?" B.J. challenged.

It was Mick's turn now to say "I don't know," and he didn't like it. He pulled the car into the police station parking lot and climbed out, then leaned down to look back into the car when B.J. didn't move. "Coming?"

"Not going to answer my question?"

"No. Are you coming?"

She jerked open the door. "Do I have a choice?"

He smiled. "Well, if you'd rather, you could sit here until I come back out."

"Thanks." B.J. threw him a scathing look and stalked across the parking lot toward the entrance. Mick followed, all the while telling himself he shouldn't be looking at the sexy way her rear moved when she walked. He cursed under his breath as it suddenly felt as if his jeans were shrinking again. He was on the verge of being mutilated by denim. Another few minutes of this and he'd be a eunuch. The minute he entered the building he waved at the desk sergeant and made a hurried detour toward the men's bathroom. There was no shower he could dive into so he did the next best thing: splashed cold water onto his face, neck, arms, even his chest, and ordered himself to stop playing the fool.

It worked. Either that, or it was the mere fact that B.J. was out of sight. Mick walked back into the station and saw B.J. talking with Detective Jarrett while propped on the corner of his desk. A flash of jealousy swept through Mick so swiftly, and so unexpectedly, that it nearly obliterated everything else from his mind.

"There's a report from the coroner," B.J. said, turning to him.

Shock at his own reaction to seeing her with Jarrett held him frozen in place.

She handed him the report. "Nothing new though."

Mick forced himself to reach out and take the report from her. He was a professional, he reminded himself, and he wasn't really interested in B.J. Poydras. Forcing

Tricks of the Trade

his mind back to business, he went over the report quickly and was just about to toss it back onto Jarrett's desk when he noticed something he hadn't seen before. "Wait a minute," Mick said.

Jarrett and B.J. stopped talking and looked at him.

"Charbonneau had false teeth?"

Jarrett shuffled several pieces of paper on his desk before coming up with another copy of the report B.J. had handed Mick. He scanned it quickly. "Looks that way. So what?"

"So what is that they were missing from the body. Was this on here before?" Mick demanded.

Jarrett shrugged. "I don't know. Why? What in the hell are you getting at, Gentry?"

Mick felt as if his blood pressure had jumped at least twenty points. "Townsend has false teeth."

"So do thousands of other people," B.J. said.

"But thousands of other people aren't involved in this case," Mick said, almost grinding out the words, "Townsend and Charbonneau are."

"So they both had false teeth," Jarrett said. He grabbed the report and looked at it. "I still don't get it."

"Look, we can't get fingerprints off the dead guy because he was burned to a crisp, right?" Mick said.

Jarrett nodded.

"But he had false teeth, like Townsend, and they're missing. Why are they missing?" He went on before they could answer. "Because somebody doesn't want us to be able to identify our John Doe as anyone other than Theodore Charbonneau, that's why."

"But it is Charbonneau," B.J. argued. "The coroner

said the body has all the physical characteristics needed to ID it as Charbonneau—height, weight, bone structure—and he was found at Charbonneau's cabin."

"And Calamity Jane is buried next to Wild Bill Hickok," Mick said with a snarl, "but that doesn't mean the two of them were really lovers."

B.J. and Jarrett stared at Mick as if they thought he'd suddenly gone crazy.

"What's that supposed to mean?" B.J. asked, finally able to get her gaping jaw working again.

"It means," Mick said after a sigh of impatience, "that you can't always believe what is the easiest thing to believe. What some people want you to believe. Sometimes you've got to look past the rumors, even past the evidence." He looked at the detective. "Can you run a check on Evie Strindel, Jarrett? Local and FBI?"

"Sure, but it'll take awhile."

"Fine." Mick turned to B.J. "Ready to go?"

She nodded. Finally. She'd see what Alice had found out, if anything, while B.J. had been away from the office. Then she'd return any phone calls that had come in about ChiChi. Once done with that she'd take Beaujolais, go home, soak in a hot tub, heat up a little gumbo, crash, and forget all about Mick Gentry and his wild theories and passion-stirring, blood-boiling, aching-to-get-her-hands-on-it, sexy body.

But once outside Mick didn't head for the car. Instead, he took her arm, gently but firmly, and steered her in the opposite direction.

B.J. dug her heels into the pavement and turned

toward him. "Just where do you think you're steering me?"

"Dinner," he said simply.

"Dinner," she echoed, slapping both hands onto her hips. "Is that supposed to be an invitation, Marshal? Because if it is, I hate to be the one to tell you, but you need to work on your presentation. And anyway, it's a little early for dinner, and I have work to do, a case to solve, and . . ."

"And you need to work on your acceptance speech," Mick countered.

"That would only be if I intended to accept."

Would anyone notice, he wondered suddenly, if he wrapped his hands around that long column of neck and strangled her right there in front of the police station? Or if he dragged her up against him, stripped her clothes away, and made mad, passionate love to her on the sidewalk?

His breath suddenly felt trapped in his throat, and his mouth was as dry as the desert at high noon. Her lips looked more delicious than anything he'd ever seen in his life. He ordered his body to calm down, and it refused to listen. Mick wanted to tell himself that it was all due to temper, that he was so annoyed, so infuriated with her that he couldn't stand it, but he knew that wasn't the truth. Oh, he was annoyed with her all right, she seemed to have the knack to keep him continually annoyed, but he suspected his reactions to her had little to nothing to do with anger and a lot to do with desire, because if truth be told he wasn't really hungry for food, he was hungry for her.

He swallowed hard and looked straight into her eyes. "So, you're turning me down?"

B.J. smiled, then wished she hadn't when she saw the challenge in his eyes. He was asking her about a lot more than dinner. "Yes. No. I mean . . ." B.J. could have bitten off her own tongue. What in the world was she doing? She didn't want to go out to dinner with him. She didn't want to go anywhere with him. So why hadn't she stuck with yes and said she was turning him down? It seemed like ever since she'd met him her mouth had been saying things that were in direct conflict with what she thought it should be saying. She'd never had that problem before. She'd always said exactly what she was thinking.

"So just what are you saying?" Mick asked, the urge to strangle her starting to get an edge over the urge to drag her into his arms and capture that delectably tantalizing mouth with his own.

"We can go to dinner," B.J. said, "and talk about the case. Business."

"Oh happy day," Mick said, rolling his eyes.

B.J. had started to turn and walk toward the car again but stopped at his words and looked back at him. "You had other plans?"

An image of her lying naked on a bed popped into his head, her skin moist and shiny with the perspiration of desire, her lips swollen with passion, her arms beckoning him to take her. Mick nearly groaned at the stabbing ache that hit his groin at the same time the image formed in his mind. He stiffened against the sensation, shifted his weight from one foot to the other, and hoped she didn't notice that he had a problem. It hadn't been that long since he'd been with a woman, but obviously his body didn't remember. Besides, when he'd decided to use B.J. Poydras, taking her to his bed hadn't exactly been what he'd had in mind. It wasn't ethical, and if he kept telling himself that, maybe his body would listen and he'd get through this evening, this case, without his blood overboiling or his private parts being crushed by his pants. "No," he growled at her finally, a little more gruffly than he had intended, "talking about the case is exactly what I had in mind."

Somehow B.J. didn't believe that, but the idea that he'd intended something a lot more personal than a business dinner didn't cause her to reconsider going with him. Instead she found herself looking forward to it, and that put a scare into her that made her tremble and wonder if, as her mother was fond of saying, she actually was crazy. After all, what could she possibly find attractive about Mick Gentry—other than his body, his face, that deep, midnight drawl, and the sexy way he walked, kind of like a swagger?

B.J. slapped a metal clamp on her runaway thoughts. Business, she reminded herself. They were going to dinner and they were going to talk business, which was all she was interested in.

EIGHT

Mick reached for the salt shaker the same time B.J. did. His fingers brushed against hers and he experienced a sudden desire to seize her and hold on, to slide his hand up her arm, touch her face, pull her toward him, and cover her lips with his.

She met his gaze. "Excuse me."

He jerked his hand back. Whatever was wrong with him, these feelings he was having toward her were becoming troublesome. He'd never reacted to a woman the way he had been reacting to B.J. Poydras, and he didn't remember ever wanting a woman as badly as he'd finally been forced to admit to himself that he wanted her. His mind instantly conjured up an erotic image of her, and he just as instantly pulled the curtain on it.

They'd talked about the case on the way to the restaurant, while they had a before-dinner drink, while they waited for their dinner to be served, and while eating their salads. Now they were midway through their main courses, had gone over just about every aspect of the case that was possible to go over, including theories, probabilities, and strategies, and both had finally run out of things to say regarding Charbonneau and Townsend. Silence floated between them.

"Ever worked on a murder case?" Mick asked, striving to make small talk and break the silence that was starting to annoy him. That in itself was unusual. He normally didn't talk much and preferred silence, which was another reason he liked to work alone.

B.J. looked up. "If you're asking if I ever get anything besides lost animal cases, Marshal, the answer is yes." Indignation burned within her breast.

"I didn't mean that."

"Yes, you did." She was being unreasonable, and she knew it. But she couldn't help it. He did that to her. "And for your information, Marshal, I consider Mrs. Charbonneau's case a valid one, and not because she's paying me good money. She loves that dog just as much as someone else might love a child."

Mick nodded. "Most likely," he mumbled.

"And I don't find anything weird about that."

He looked up at her, frowning. "I didn't say there was anything weird about it."

"You were thinking it."

He set his fork down, and a crooked smile pulled at one corner of his mouth as he looked at her. "So, you're psychic now?"

She threw her napkin onto the table. "You don't have to bother walking me to my car." She rose. "It's only a few blocks."

"Far enough to get mugged," Mick said, tossing enough money onto the table to cover the check and tip.

She smiled, but it was anything but warm. "I know how to take care of myself, Marshal. I have a brown belt." She also had a gun.

"Wouldn't do you much good if the guy who attacked you was a black belt, now would it?" Mick stood. He didn't know why he was playing this game, letting her anger goad him and his own emotions overrule his better sense. She'd given him an out and he should have taken it. But then, she'd given him half a dozen outs since they'd met, and he hadn't taken any of them. "I'll walk you to your car."

"I told you, it's not necessary."

"I'll walk you to your car," he repeated.

Five minutes later they arrived at B.J.'s car, without encountering another soul on the street, good or bad, but Mick knew that didn't mean no one was there. Muggers were rarely noticed until it was too late, and there were so many places in the French Quarter a mugger could hide—ancient alleyways, time-worn porte cocheres, arched doorways, and shadowed shop entrances—that, after dark, it could be a virtual Shangri-la for muggers.

B.J. unlocked the driver's door of her car. "Well, good night." She slid onto the seat, secured her seat belt, pulled the door closed, and turned the ignition key, all without another glance at Mick, who remained standing beside the door. The engine whirred sickly. B.J. tried it again. The whir was shorter. She tried again. This time nothing at all happened.

She unsnapped her seat belt, threw open the door, and climbed out, standing to glare at the car.

"Battery's dead," Mick said.

B.J. slapped a hand against the roof of the car. "But how could it be? Nothing was left on."

"Maybe it just gave up."

"That can't be it," B.J. snapped. "This car is almost brand new." She got out, walked to the front of the car, and opened the hood.

Mick moved to stand beside her and looked into the engine, dimly illuminated by a nearby streetlight. "Well, your car may be almost brand new, but I'd say that battery has a few years on it. Like, quite a few. Maybe twenty or thirty."

B.J. moved to his side and looked down at the object in question. Rust and years of dirt, grime, and grease clung to the battery.

"But how can this be?" B.J. wailed.

Mick shrugged and slammed the hood closed. "Someone switched with you. Took your newer one, left you his old one. Come on." He took her arm. "I'll take you home and you can call someone to come fix this in the morning."

When they arrived at B.J.'s condo overlooking Lake Pontchartrain, she was no calmer than she had been the moment she'd learned someone had stolen her car's battery. Mick had tried to talk to her during the short drive, but her curt, snapped-off, angry responses had soon pushed him into silence, and her into an even darker mood.

B.J. stalked toward the door to her unit, digging in her purse for her keys. Now she had a case that could make her the laughingstock of the city and that she was getting nowhere with, and a U.S. marshal glued to her side that sent her pulse racing and caused her to have the most erotic daydreams she'd ever had in her life, and someone had broken into her car and stolen her battery. So what next? She'd walk into her apartment, find it ransacked, and Beaujolais shaved head to toe?

She unlocked her front door and was immediately reassured when she saw Beaujolais prancing toward her without a hair missing. As he romped about her feet, B.J. held onto the doorknob and turned back to Mick. Asking him in and offering him coffee was the polite thing to do. It was also the last thing in the world she wanted to do. She didn't want him in her home, she was in no mood to be polite, and she didn't want to make coffee. "Well, thanks and good—"

His beeper went off, and the unexpected loud sound made her jump nearly a foot.

Mick grinned. "Sorry. It hardly ever sounds, but when it does, the agency wants to make certain we hear it." He reached under his jacket and flipped it off.

"Oh, ah, well, you can use my phone," she said, stepping back and pointing to it on the table next to the couch. She flipped the light switch, and the room was filled with a soft glow from overhead track lights.

"Thanks." He walked past her and picked up the receiver, punching out his number.

Tricks of the Trade

Were the Fates against her? she wondered. Had they brought him into her life to tease and punish her for something she wasn't even aware she'd done?

She closed the front door and lay her bag on a nearby table. Eavesdropping was rude, but he was in her house. She paused near the doorway to the living room, hesitant, then entered.

"Yeah, right," he said, glancing at her. "Okay." He hung up and immediately started to dial another number.

She looked around, wondering what she should do with herself. With a long sigh she headed for the kitchen. "Would you like some coffee?"

He hooked the receiver under his chin. "Love some." Turning then, he cradled the receiver between his ear and shoulder and mumbled into it. Retrieving a notebook and pen from his pocket, he began jotting something down and nodding as he listened.

B.J. was being eaten alive by curiosity, as well as apprehension at having him in her apartment. She was just carrying the coffee into the room when he hung up the phone.

"Important?" she said, deciding to find out just how much her new "partner" was going to share with her.

"Maybe, maybe not," he said lightly, reaching for his coffee. His gaze strayed over her from head to toe and he felt his blood start to warm. It was a danger sign, but one he chose to ignore for the moment.

She waited silently, not about to ask " 'maybe or maybe not' what?" and telling herself she'd been right all along. He was just like all the others. He didn't intend to tell her any more than he had to, and obviously he felt he didn't have to tell her what the phone call was about.

"I was beeped by my division's secretary at headquarters. I asked her to double-check and make certain that Townsend's cousin really was dead. It was a long shot but . . ." He shrugged.

B.J. sat in a chair, sipped her coffee, and tried to hide her surprise, then reassured herself that he was only telling her what was probably unimportant anyway.

"Carl's cousin was named Jason. Jason was in on the robberies. He drove the getaway car a couple of times and was their mastermind at scouting out the locations, getting timetables on the employees, their habits, and so on. The district attorney had planned to try them separately, but Jason was killed in an accident before his trial date came up." Mick sipped his coffee. "And their other partner died in the pen." He held up the cup. "Good coffee."

"Thanks. So, they verified Jason is dead?"

"As much as possible. The car he was driving plowed into a camper and it blew up upon impact. Jason and the guy in the camper were fried."

"Just like Theodore Charbonneau," B.J. said.

Mick frowned. "Yeah."

She looked at him, wondering suddenly what it would be like to sleep cradled in his arms. The thought shocked her, and she took a long gulp of coffee, nearly choking. When she'd finished coughing, and feeling like a fool, she settled quietly back into her chair. Obviously he was not going to tell her about the second phone call.

"The clerk at headquarters told me I had a message

a my machine from Jarrett, so I called him," Mick said. "He claims a street informant heard that a couple has put out word they need some fake ID papers and a private charter to Bermuda."

"And you think this is related," B.J. said, forcing herself to concentrate on business. It wasn't a question—she felt certain that's exactly what he thought.

He nodded. "I think it's either Townsend and Evie, or Charbonneau and Evie."

"Why?"

"Because we're pretty certain at least either Charbonneau or Townsend is still alive, and I've got a feeling Evie is involved in this thing up to her neck."

"So what do we do?" B.J. said.

"Wait."

He'd surprised her again. He didn't impress her as a man who liked to wait—for anything. She had figured he'd want to go out and talk to Jarrett's informant, then start scouring the street in search of the couple in question. "For what?" she asked.

"Jarrett's informant is going to keep him abreast of what happens, and let him know if it looks like these two are actually going to get the papers."

B.J. nodded.

Mick knew he should leave, but found that he didn't want to. "Tell me about yourself," he said, seeing the surprise that came into her eyes with his attempt to change the subject. He was playing with fire, walking on the wild side, shooting himself in the foot, and he couldn't seem to help it.

"I already have."

"What's B.J. stand for?"

"Belinda Janelle." The moment she said her name she wished she could grab the words and stuff them back into her mouth. She never, ever told anyone what her name was. Even in grammar school she'd hated it so much, she hadn't told a soul. And once, in second grade, when a substitute teacher had called her by name, she'd refused to answer. That had gotten her a trip to the principal, who had threatened to call her mother if she didn't answer by her name next time she was addressed by it. B.J. refused to be Belinda Janelle. And now she might as well have told the entire NOPD.

"Belinda Janelle," Mick said, rolling the name slowly off of his tongue. "That's pretty. So why do you just go by initials?"

"Easier," B.J. lied.

"Belle."

She cringed. "B.J.," she said.

"I like Belle."

She pushed out of her chair. "B.J. or nothing."

He rose and followed her into the kitchen. "Okay, B.J., you win . . . for now."

Three hours later they were still talking. By now B.J. had told him almost everything there was to know about B.J. Poydras. As the clock on her mantel showed that it was nearly midnight, she realized she had still learned very little about him, his answers to her questions always proving either very short or totally evasive.

"So, Marshal," she said, "what's your story? I know

you're a marshal, you have a ranch in Nevada, and an ex. . . ." The word "wife" stuck in her throat like a cork in a champagne bottle. No, she didn't want to go in that direction, did she?

Yes, a little voice in the back of her mind whispered.

No, she promptly answered back.

"Wife," he supplied. "That's just about my story, B.J. My work keeps me on the road almost constantly, which isn't conducive to marriage. I spend maybe five or six days a month on my ranch, my parents are dead, I was an only child, and I have no cousins, aunts, or uncles because my parents were also both only children. Short story," he said flippantly.

B.J. felt an unwelcome heat stealing into her cheeks. "Ever been to New Orleans before?" she asked, deciding to get onto a safer subject.

"I would have thought the answer to that was pretty obvious."

"So, tell me what it's like to live on a ranch," she said. "Your kids must love it." Where had that come from? Little ripples of shock swept through B.J., followed by a crashing wave of mortification. If she could have crawled under the sofa, she would have. Immediately.

He smiled, but she saw a glimmer of sadness in his eyes. What did it mean? The heat in her cheeks was burning to the point that she felt certain her entire face was crimson.

He rose and walked across the room, pausing with his back to her to stand at the glass doors that led to the balcony and gave view of Lake Pontchartrain across the street.

She looked at the slant of his shoulders and noticed there seemed to be a slight sag to them that wasn't there before. She wondered suddenly if his wife had died, and felt a sense of guilt for having brought up the subject. B.J. rose and moved to stand beside him. "I'm sorry," she said softly. "It's none of my business."

He turned and stared down at her as if attempting to penetrate through the barriers B.J. kept erected around herself and invade her soul.

He had kissed her before, and she'd nearly lost herself to him then. For hours afterward she had felt unstable, as if no longer grounded in reality, as if her world had suddenly tilted and she didn't know how to set it straight. And now he was going to do it again, and B.J. knew she wasn't going to do anything to stop him.

It was insane. He was everything she'd always tried to avoid, exactly the type of man she'd sworn never to become involved with. He was hard, rugged, self-righteous and determined, arrogant, stubborn, and opinionated. She sensed, with a certainty beyond doubt, that he was a man who would stop at nothing to get what he wanted. A man who would let nothing and no one stand in his way.

She needed a man who knew how to compromise. A man who was gentle, sophisticated, and open-minded. A man who would respect her for who and what she was, and not try to make her change.

Yet even as her consciousness registered all this, even as his hands reached for her, touched her waist, and slid around to her back, she knew it was too late to resist, too late to try to convince herself that what he was silently offering, she didn't want.

She heard the soft expletive that left his lips, no louder than a whisper on the wind, and knew that he was cursing his own defeat as much as she was chagrined by hers.

Her body trembled from the force of emotions stirred by his touch, and when his head lowered toward her, when his mouth touched the side of her neck, his lips like flame, burning into her flesh, she moaned aloud and slipped her arms around his neck, dragging him closer. There was no longer enough will left in B.J. to enable her to deny what she'd wanted from the moment he'd walked into her office. His virility drew her to him like a magnet. His gazes felt like soft caresses, his touches like flickers of fire.

Tomorrow she might damn herself, curse him, and rail against the situation that had brought them together, but not tonight. His hands slid up her back, crushing her against his chest, and the very air around them seemed suddenly to become electrified. A shiver of want swept through her, accelerating her pulse, intensifying the heat of passion that had invaded every cell of her body, and leaving her helpless in its wake.

His hands were warm and vibrant as they moved beneath her blouse to glide tenderly over her back.

"I thought one kiss would be enough," he said, his voice deep and rough against the curve of her neck, "but I was wrong." His mouth swooped to capture hers, as the hawk captures the dove. His kiss awakened such heated sensitivity and longing that B.J.'s lips parted in a surprised gasp of pleasure, and Mick took instant advantage, his tongue slipping into the dark recesses of her mouth to taste her desire.

B.J. clung to him, each demanding, hungry stroke of his tongue matched by one of her own. As had happened before when he'd kissed her, fireworks seemed to explode within her, one burst of flame after another, but this time his kisses were fiercer, more demanding, each attacking the barriers she'd built around herself, around her wants and needs, exposing a raw craving of desire so strong, so intense, she knew it had to be satisfied or she would die.

His mouth was hard and hot on hers, hungry in its assault, demanding in its caress. She felt his need in that kiss, and an agony of loneliness that surprised her.

Raising his mouth from hers, he gazed deep into her eyes, not moving, still holding her crushed against him, yet waiting, she sensed, for her to demand he release her.

When she didn't, his features seemed to relax. He raised a hand to her face and, as his fingers traced the curve of her cheek, she found his touch almost unbearable in its tenderness. "I need you," he said softly, emotion deepening his voice. "I want to make love to you."

NINE

"I know," B.J. whispered, burying her face in his neck and pressing her lips to the soft flesh there, "and I want you to make love to me."

She felt the heady sensation of his lips against her neck, each caress sending new spirals of ecstasy through her, each warm velvet touch causing her passion to deepen, her desire for him to intensify. Her boldness surprised her, her emotions urging her on, something that had never happened with another man. B.J. turned her head toward him, and his mouth recaptured hers, his kiss by turns as light as a summer breeze and as hard and demanding as a winter storm.

His passion rose with hers, his body growing ever harder under the touch of her roaming, exploring hands, the broad muscles of his shoulders turning to steel, his flesh turning to fire as her hands slipped between his jacket and shirt to knead and caress.

There was both an urgency and an intimacy to his kiss

that B.J. had never known before, a demand that she surrender to him, a plea that she return his fervor. She melted into him, knowing she would have been unable to resist even if she'd wanted to, succumbing to the forceful domination of his lips, and wanting it never to end.

She felt his hands move, one on her breast, the other slipping beneath the silky sheath of her blouse to release the catch of her brassiere. A soft moan slipped from her lips when his hand moved beneath the lacy cup to cradle her breast within the circle of his fingers, and an ache, so overpowering that she trembled, pierced her body. His thumb flicked over her nipple, and she leaned into him, a moan of desire ripping from her throat again, need and want boiling within her blood, stabbing at her loins, vanquishing any thoughts from her mind but those of him and the wondrous touch of his body against hers.

Mick knew he was lost to her, not as a conscious thought, but more a resolution that swept through his entire being. He had never felt such a gnawing ache of need before. It filled his entire body, demanding he sacrifice himself to it, commanding he seek satiation. He hadn't meant for this to happen, hadn't even intended to kiss her again. It was too dangerous. He knew, even though he hadn't wanted to admit it, that she'd touched him emotionally where he hadn't let anyone touch him in years. She'd made him start to feel again, start to want things he'd never thought he would want again. Yet instead of running from her, instead of fleeing for his very life, for his sanity, he'd put himself in this situation, and he knew now it was because he'd really had no choice. He wanted B.J. more than he'd ever wanted any woman.

Tricks of the Trade

There was no turning back, and there was no denying that fact. With the thin thread of reason still left to him, he wondered if he would even survive this encounter, if once he made love to her, he would be able to go back to life the way he knew it.

If he'd been any kind of man at all, any kind of gentleman, Mick knew he would stop right then, pull away from her, apologize, and leave. But pulling away from her, let alone leaving, was not an option. It was not something he could force himself to do. Not now. Not anymore.

His hand slid down between their bodies to her waist, to the clasp of her slacks, and with a deft twist of his fingers, he released it.

B.J. felt the silk material slip from her hips, felt it flutter past her thighs and fall to the floor around her ankles, but she was too lost in his kiss to care or even contemplate resistance. This was what she wanted, and there was no longer any reason or will within her to deny it.

As his lips continued their ravishing assault upon her mouth, and one hand continued to caress her bared breast, his other moved to the front of her blouse and released its small white buttons. His hand left her breast then, and B.J. felt suddenly bereft, deserted. She moaned a protest, the sound slipping from her mouth to be swallowed by his.

Mick's hands moved up her arms, gently pulled hers from around his neck, and guided them downward to her sides as he pushed the blouse from her shoulders.

His lips left hers and pressed against her neck, grazed

the lobe of her ear, settled in the hollow of her throat. He slipped her panties from her hips and his mouth moved to her breast, across her stomach, and finally, as he knelt, he pressed his lips into the small triangle that was revealed to him as the pale blue silk panty left her thighs.

B.J.'s legs trembled violently at the intimacy of his act, a stab of pleasure shooting through her like a lightning bolt, and she thought she was going to faint. His tongue touched the sensitive tip that was the core of her passion, and his name ripped from her lips in a half groan, half plea. She wanted to implore him to stop before she fell to her knees, and she wanted to beg him to continue until she breathed her last breath.

Rising, Mick dragged her back into his embrace. "You're so beautiful, B.J.," he whispered against her neck, "and I want you so much."

He kissed her then with a fiery passion that sent her senses reeling into a place filled with darkness and stars, moonbeams and rainbows, and she responded to his seduction of her more eagerly, more wantonly, than she'd ever imagined she could. At that moment B.J. was certain Mick Gentry was not merely a man. He was the culmination of every carnal thought she'd ever had, the reality of all her erotic fantasies. Every inch of her body craved the touch of his hands, passion moved through her like fire over a dry prairie, and awareness of him invaded her senses to such a degree that nothing else mattered, nothing else even existed but that he remain with her, that he continue his assault on her passions, that he make love to her.

Mick knew B.J. was the embodiment of every dream

and nightmare he'd ever had since the day Sherry had left him. And he'd known it since that first talk he'd had with B.J. in her office. This awareness had lived in the back of his mind since that moment, hovered there, waiting to sneak out, to make him do exactly what he was doing now, to make him feel again. Feeling again, being vulnerable to another person, to his own feelings, wasn't what he wanted, yet he knew that if he denied himself being with her, if he walked away now, he would go slowly mad with longing.

And walking away was something he couldn't make himself do.

He started to lower her to the floor, then paused when he felt B.J. resist. Everything in him screamed no, she couldn't pull away from him now.

She dragged her lips from his. "No," she whispered. "Wait."

His heart nearly stopped, his breath, ragged and choking, caught in his throat, and it took every ounce of willpower Mick possessed to still his hands and keep himself from raging out at her.

With a devilish gleam in her eye and a sassy smile curving her lips, B.J. looked up at him. "My turn," she said softly, and, unbuttoning his shirt, slipped her hands beneath it and pushed it from his shoulders.

Relief flooded through him like the waters of a burst dam. His muscles, every fiber of his body, were already hardened to rock by his growing need of her.

Her fingers undid his belt buckle, released the snap of his jeans, then began to work his zipper downward, and all thought of the past fled from Mick's mind. She slid her hands to his hips, shoved her fingers beneath the faded, well-worn denim, and pushed them and his shorts down, letting them drop the rest of the way on their own.

Kicking off his boots, Mick stepped from his pants, laughing softly as B.J. stared down at the evidence of how badly he wanted her.

"Change your mind?" he asked softly, pulling her back against him and cupping one breast in the warmth of his hand while his arousal rested, hard and hot, against the apex of her thighs.

A sharp stab of pleasure momentarily robbed her of breath, while delicious anticipation rippled through her veins. "No," she finally managed, just as his lips descended upon hers.

They sank to the floor, their bodies instinctively fitting together, flesh to flesh. His hands moved over her length, up and down, following every curve and line, leaving searing trails wherever he touched, explored, and probed. He traced a fingertip across her bottom lip, then assaulted her with another kiss that sent delicious shivers of desire coursing through her.

Each stroke of his hands was sweet torment, fueling her need of him, teasing her desires until she knew she hovered on the brink of delirium, of needing him so badly, of wanting him so desperately, that she would do anything. B.J. slid her fingers over the strong tendons in the back of his neck, the hard muscles that spread across his shoulders, and into the thickness of his hair, twisting the golden curls around her fingers. Then, as her need for him grew ever more extreme, she grew bolder, more daring, more demanding.

Tricks of the Trade

Whatever control Mick might have had over his emotions, over his physical restraint, vanished when he felt B.J.'s hand move between them, caress his hip, then slide through the dark hairs that grew below his stomach and clasp him tenderly but firmly. His heart nearly jumped into his throat, and his need of her soared to an intensity that threatened to consume him. Her fingertips were as hot as flame as they stroked, as hot as fire as they slid up and down the length of his arousal, then moved over its sensitive tip of flesh.

"You're going to kill me," he growled against her lips, the words forced from his frame on a gasp of pleasure.

She smiled. "Then you'll die a happy man, won't you, Marshal?"

His probing tongue filled her mouth, as his hands urged her legs apart and his need filled her body.

She suddenly breathed in soul-gasping breaths as their bodies moved together, and she abandoned herself to passion, to the quest for its ultimate end.

Mick thought he had died and gone to heaven. He stared up at the ceiling, illuminated softly by a stray beam of moonlight filtering in through the glass doors beside them. B.J. lay snuggled against his chest, her head cradled in the crook of his arm. His other arm was bent under his head, acting as a pillow.

Sex with B.J. had been more than he'd bargained for, more than he'd ever experienced, more than he'd probably ever know again once he left her. But he knew he had to leave her. When he wrapped up this case, he had to go.

There was no other way. He inhaled deeply and her scent, of the night-blooming jasmine that permeated the South, filled his lungs and his senses. It was a fragrance he would never again be able to encounter without thinking of B.J.

"Belle," he whispered, and smiled.

"B.J.," she said softly.

He looked down at her. "I thought you were asleep."

She snuggled closer, fitting the contours of her body to the long, lean lines of his, slipping an arm around his waist and a leg over his thigh. "I was, for a few minutes."

"I should go," he said, not really wanting to.

"You should stay," she countered.

He smiled. "We might end up doing this again," he said, as if this were a warning or threat.

She looked up at him, a promise in her eyes. "Yes, we just might."

Mick was totally unprepared for the jolt of raw desire that hit him at the invitation in her words.

"Or, aren't you up to it, cowboy?" B.J. teased when she saw the evidence of his renewed arousal.

Before she could even guess what he was going to do or say, Mick moved to partially pin her beneath him. "Is that an invitation, lady," he said softly, "or a challenge?"

She smiled. "How about if it's both?" she said.

His mouth came down on hers instantly, claiming her acquiescence and demanding more.

And B.J. gave willingly, knowing at that moment that if he had asked for her life, she would have given him that too.

Tricks of the Trade

Nothing in life had prepared her to be with a man like Mick Gentry. A man who, she realized now as he slept beside her, was as soft as he was hard, as giving as he was demanding. She sensed he could be a hero, a villain, or a hated enemy, depending on who he was facing and what he wanted of them. While they had been making love, B.J. had unconsciously learned a lot about Mick Gentry. One thing she'd discovered was that Mick Gentry was also a man whose personality held more facets than she had ever even dreamt could exist within one human being, a man who could successfully hide behind the toughness of the persona he offered the world, but whose eyes could not hide his true feelings, if one looked closely enough to see them there.

Fortunately, or unfortunately, B.J. had looked closely enough, and what she'd seen had shocked, surprised, and saddened her. As well as she knew her own name, she knew that Mick Gentry had suffered a deep, sorrowful pain, the kind that rips a heart apart and never quite heals. It had been there in his eyes when the barriers he kept around his emotions had given way, when he'd given himself to her totally. She'd caught a hint of it that time when he'd mentioned he had been married once, but now she'd seen it in the depth of his eyes when he'd made love to her, felt it in the urgency of his kiss and the fire of his passion, and knew that whatever had happened, whoever or whatever had hurt him, it had changed Mick Gentry in some way, forever.

Snuggling deeper into his arms, B.J. closed her eyes

and willed herself to go to sleep. If Jarrett's informant was right, and Theodore—or Townsend—was still alive and was trying to get phony papers and a way out of the country with Evie, she and Mick could have a very busy day ahead of them.

B.J. sighed. How had a simple lost dog case evolved into mystery, intrigue, and murder?

And brought a U.S. marshal to her door?

Smiling, it was the last conscious thought she had before drifting off to sleep.

Mick woke with a start. He stared into the darkness, trying to orient himself as his heart thudded madly in his chest. He felt the warm flesh of another person pressed up against his right side, his arm pinned by the weight. A multitude of smells met his nostrils—woman smells, he determined. Perfume, hair spray, spices. The almost panic-stricken beat of his heart instantly began to slow, to decelerate to a more normal pace as he remembered where he was.

The attack, the sensation of being held helpless while danger moved stealthily all around him, had been coming to him since the day Kyle had been taken from him. Whenever he slept, day or night, it hovered within his dreams, waited for him to stir and wake, and then it pounced, seizing his mind and body, even if only momentarily. It was something he should be used to by now, but he wasn't. He'd never get used to it, but he had learned to live with it and understand it. It had been born out of loss, and he knew the only way to keep it from becoming

Tricks of the Trade

worse, to keep himself from being ripped apart and going insane, was never to let himself love again.

He slowly slid his arm from beneath B.J., not wanting to wake her, and pushed himself off of the floor. Pulling on his jeans, he grabbed B.J.'s phone from the coffee table and moved into the kitchen, dialing as he walked. It was too early, or late, for anyone to be in the office, but he could leave a message. When voice mail answered, Mick punched the number for his department's secretary.

"Tina, this is Mick. I need you to do something first thing when you come in. I want you to do another check on Carl Townsend's background, and this time find out anything and everything you can about his cousin Jason, the one who died in that car accident. Then see if there are any other relatives, and if he ever knew anyone named Evie Strindel. And while you're at it, do a check on Evie Strindel and Theodore Charbonneau." He paused, trying to think if he'd forgotten anything. He gave his secretary B.J.'s number, then he thought better of having her use it. "Don't beep me, Tina, or call me, I'll call you back." Mick disconnected and walked back into the living room. He stopped in the middle of the room and looked down at B.J., who had turned onto her side and was still sleeping.

"You're a fool," Mick said to himself. He moved past her to stand at the window. Sunlight was just beginning to invade the darkness of the night and transform the lake's moonlit surface from a sheet of silver to a slate of gold. His ex-wife's parting words suddenly sounded, all too loud and clear, in Mick's mind. "You were rotten father material, and even worse as a husband." His mother had tried to tell him that Sherry had only been lashing out because of pain and anger, that it wasn't true, that what had happened wasn't his fault. But Mick knew differently. He hadn't been the kind of father Kyle had deserved, and he had never been the kind of husband Sherry had wanted.

Glancing down at B.J., Mick knew the best thing he could do for her now, and for himself, was to stop this thing that was growing between them before it got any more out of hand. It had already gone far beyond what it should have, and that was his fault too.

Bending down to retrieve his shirt, he paused as B.J. murmured, rolled over, and, as her lashes fluttered open, held out her arms to him. "Come here and arrest me, Marshal," she said, a sassy, teasing lilt to her voice.

In spite of himself, Mick smiled.

Darkness still hovered about the room, but the blending light of the moon and rising sun drifted faintly through the sliding glass doors and touched her body, turning her golden skin to burnished copper, her long dark hair, fanning out loosely around her on the rug, to near ebony strands of satin that gleamed softly and beckoned his fingers to slip through them just one more time. He knew it was dangerous, but he had to kiss her again, a last time, to say good-bye. Then he would tell her it was best they not see each other anymore, not even to work on the case, because being around her and not touching her was something he knew he would never be able to do again. There was no future for them, there could never be for anyone with Mick. She deserved a man who could give her a future, and it was the one thing he knew he couldn't offer. They could work through Jarrett, each keeping him informed of their moves, intentions, and what they'd found out so as not to double the effort and cross paths. It would be better that way. He dropped to one knee beside her. "B.J., listen, I . . ."

Her arms slid around his neck, molding themselves to the corded muscles of his shoulders, and she pulled him down toward her. "I don't want to listen," she said, her voice as sultry and seductive as any he could have imagined, "I want to feel."

Before he could do more than open his mouth to protest, her lips covered his in a kiss that was at once urgent and torpid, as fleetingly hesitant as the flutter of a nightingale's wing, yet intoxicating and provocative. Her tongue moved between his parted lips like a dart of flame, burning wherever it touched, singeing his flesh and branding his soul.

Mick felt shivers of desire wrack his body, felt his resistance to her touch, his resolve to walk away from her, desert him like so much smoke on the wind. Her kiss, and all the feelings within her that he knew were behind it, were like a salve to his tortured spirit, a balm that momentarily chased away the loneliness that was his everyday companion. Even so, there was a thread of reason still left in him, a thin tendril of decency still left within his reach, and Mick knew he had to grasp it and force himself to do the right thing, to walk away from her now, before he hurt her the way he had Sherry.

Placing his hands on the floor, one to each side of her head, he was about to push himself upward, to pull away from her, when he felt one of her hands slip within his still unzipped jeans and wrap around the arousal he had been so desperately trying to ignore. A deep groan rumbled from his throat, sounding both his defeat and his surrender. Heaven help him, he could no sooner leave her at this moment than he could refuse himself another breath, and all he could do was pray that when he did finally find the resolve to leave her, she wouldn't really care.

At the same time, the thought that their sharing was merely a physical release for her was not only one he found himself unable to accept, but one that caused an emptiness to suddenly invade a heart long walled off from any kind of warm feelings.

Yet even as he was forced to acknowledge, however grudgingly, that he was losing a part of himself to her, he knew there was nothing he could do about it. He knew that in the months to come, after he was long gone from her life, he would remember this time with her, remember the feelings she had caused to resurface within him, and the loneliness would be more intense because of it. But that was the price he would have to pay . . . the price he was willing to pay. For now, just for a little while, he would allow himself to feel again, and hope that if he caused her any hurt at all, it was a fleeting thing, and one that would not go too deeply.

The first time they had made love it had been hot, demanding, mind-searing passion. The second time it had been slower, more intimate, a seductive and mutual exploration. This time, for Mick, it had been a torment sweeter than any he had ever known, made all the more poignant by the knowledge that it would be the last time with her.

Yet even as they lay together, the heat of their passion covering their bodies and gleaming in the rays of the steadily rising sun, Mick couldn't bring himself to leave.

He moved slightly and looked down at B.J., snuggled tightly against him, her head resting on his shoulder. She deserved better, he told himself, every curse he'd ever heard racing through his mind, every foul name and derogatory label that could be directed at himself echoing through his thoughts.

Things had already gone too far between them, and it was all his fault. He should have kept her at arm's length, should never have asked her to dinner, driven her home, come into her apartment. He hadn't needed to use her phone. He had his own, a small cellular he carried in his jacket pocket. He'd inadvertently left it in the car, hadn't had it with him when his beeper went off, but it would have taken only a minute to tell her good-bye and get to the car and the phone. Guilt slammed into him, but he didn't try to shrug it off, because he knew he deserved to feel it, deserved to suffer under its assault.

Mick started to pull his arm from beneath her, intent on rising, dressing, and leaving. If she woke before he left, he'd apologize, tell her they couldn't see each other anymore, tell her he was a bastard, that he was unable to feel, to love. He'd tell her whatever was necessary to make her turn away from him. The one thing he wouldn't tell her was the truth.

Before he had moved more than an inch, the jangling

bell of the telephone sounded, splitting the silence as effectively as a snap of lightning.

B.J. bolted up, glanced at him, then grabbed for the phone he'd returned to its place on the coffee table. "Mick Gentry?" she murmured after listening to the caller for a second.

Mick saw a coolness suddenly fall over her features as she turned and handed the telephone to him.

"It's for you. Your office."

He took the phone and listened as Tina apologized for calling rather than waiting for him to call, but explained that she was leaving for the rest of the day and wanted to make certain he got the information he'd requested. She'd faxed it to Detective Jarrett's attention at NOPD with instructions to hold it for Mick.

Hanging up, Mick turned to find himself alone in the living room. Grabbing his pants, he shoved his foot into one pant leg.

"How dare you," B.J. spat out, burning with indignation as she stepped back into the room, dressed in a pale lavender jogging suit, her dark hair pulled back and secured in a ponytail. Barely bridled anger flashed from her eyes.

"How dare I what?" Mick echoed, totally baffled not only by her statement but by her sudden anger.

B.J. glared at him, so angry she could hardly breathe. "How dare you what?" she flared, nearly choking on the words.

"Yes," Mick said, "how dare I what?"

She trembled from the force of her own anger and indignation. "You gave my phone number out," she snapped. "You . . . you assumed you would be spending the night here, and told them to call here this morning."

He opened his mouth to deny her accusation, to explain, but she cut him off.

"Is that your normal modus operandi, Marshal? Weasel your way into someone's life, con your way into her case, then use her any and every way you can?" B.J. threw up her hands, whirled around, then whirled back toward him again. "I can't believe I was such a fool. I never learn. Never, never, never." She grabbed her keys, a can of pepper spray, and a pair of dark glasses from the breakfast bar. "Don't be here when I get back, Marshal."

"B.J., I—" Mick cut the protest off. Not because the look she threw back at him was cold enough to freeze the dead, but because he suddenly realized that what had just happened was probably for the best. She'd hate him now, think he was the lowest of the low. Was that any different than what she would think of him if he had gone through with what he'd planned and simply walked out of her life with an apology for entering it, making love to her, and then saying there could be no more? Maybe, he mused, it was better this way, letting her be the one to break it off; maybe she'd hurt less this way.

Sherry had been right, he thought, for probably the millionth time since he'd last seen her four years before.

"Come on, Beaujolais," B.J. called. The tiny dog bounded out from her bedroom and slipped through the open door after her. She slammed it shut, and Mick pulled on his other pant leg.

Yes, it was better this way. He had work to do, and after he caught Townsend, there would be another case that needed him, and then another and another. But even as he told himself this, he suddenly realized with dismay that he didn't really care if he ever caught Carl Townsend, if the world kept rotating, or if he even breathed another breath.

Mick stiffened against the traitorous feelings. He did care, dammit, he had to care. He had to. It was the only world he had. It was his life.

The screech of skidding tires broke into his thoughts. A woman's scream nearly stopped his heart.

TEN

B.J. stalked away from her condo, staring at the beach across the street, seeing it without really seeing it. "The audacity of the man," she swore softly, "leaving my phone number around because he assumed he was going to spend the night with me." She felt like punching something. "Assumed he was going to sleep with me," she repeated, this time making no effort to keep her voice down. "And I let him do it. Aghh." B.J. silently called herself every kind of fool she could think of.

Beaujolais pranced beside her, occasionally stopping to sniff at something in the grass beside the walkway.

"Boy, I can really pick 'em, can't I, Beau?" she grumbled. "It's as obvious as the nose on my face that I'm a rotten judge of character when it comes to men, so why don't I just stay away from them? Forget 'em? I mean, look how many times I've been engaged. That should have told me something, right?" She threw her arms up in disgust, then jerked a pair of dark glasses from her pocket and slammed them onto her face. "But oh no, not me. I don't learn that easy. I have to be made a fool of in front of the entire New Orleans police department."

She was so mad, and getting madder by the second, that she didn't pause when Beaujolais stopped at the curb and barked. "If you're coming, then come on," she called over her shoulder, and walked into the street. "I'm not carrying you."

Beaujolais barked again.

B.J. stopped and turned back to him. "I said, either come or go ho—" She caught a blur of black out of the corner of her eye and, her heart suddenly seized by fear, knew instinctively what was about to happen. With a scream ripping from her throat, she dived for the curb, even though she knew she was much too far from it to reach it.

The car's left fender caught her thigh, and pain, searing, hot, and unbearable, ripped through her body. The force of the impact hurled her through the air.

She heard Beaujolais bark again and prayed that she wouldn't land on him, that her parents would forgive her for dying, that she could see Mick Gentry's face just one more time. She landed on the hood of a parked car, then tumbled to the ground. The world mercifully clicked off then and left her with nothing but blackness.

Beaujolais's frantic barks filled the air as he wiggled around B.J.'s unconscious form, nuzzling her as if trying to make her wake up.

"B.J.," Mick yelled, slamming open the door of her condo and running toward her. Fear turned his legs wooden and his flesh cold. This was all his fault. Just like with Kyle, just like with Sherry, it was all his fault. He dropped down beside B.J. and reached out for her, then stopped, afraid to touch her, afraid he would hurt her more, if that was even possible. He looked down at her unconscious form, his own hands trembling, his heart threatening to burst through his chest. Blood seeped from a gash on her forehead, and she suddenly looked paler to him than any person he'd ever seen.

Tears filled Mick's eyes and he brusquely blinked them away, cursing them, cursing himself. He looked around. Several other people from the condo complex had come outside at hearing the commotion. "Call an ambulance," Mick yelled at the gathering crowd. "Someone call an ambulance."

He saw several people whirl and race for their doors. "B.J.," he whispered, looking down at her again. "B.J." But she didn't move, didn't open her eyes. He leaned down to her, listening for her breathing, and found it ragged. He felt the pulse in her neck—slow. Panic threatened to overtake him. There was no time to wait for an ambulance. It didn't appear that she had any broken bones, but he wasn't a doctor, and she could have internal injuries, could be slipping away from him even as he looked down at her.

"No." The word, whispered as part protest, part plea, slipped from his lips unbidden, even unnoticed.

"Is she dead, mister?"

Mick turned to glare up at the little boy who'd ventured near. He was no more than five, his eyes wide with curiosity.

"My mom got hit by a car, and she's living with the angels now. My grand-mère said so."

Mick looked back down at B.J. She couldn't die. A knot of emotion caught in his throat. She couldn't die. He slid his arms under her and, praying he didn't hurt her further, scooped her up. He couldn't take a chance on waiting, couldn't take the risk that the ambulance wouldn't arrive in time to help her, that by waiting for the paramedics they'd lose valuable time and would get to the hospital too late.

Rising, Mick cradled B.J. against his chest and hurried toward his car, gulping back his own fears, praying that this time he wouldn't be too late, that this time the Fates wouldn't be so cruel.

One of the neighbors, a gray-haired woman in a pink robe, scurried forth to grab the little boy's hand and open the back door of Mick's car for him. He climbed in and lay B.J. on the seat, quickly covering her with the jacket he'd left there the previous night. Beaujolais jumped in between Mick's feet and scrambled across the floor to huddle against the seat near B.J.'s head. A soft whine rippled from his throat and his big brown eyes looked glassy, as if he was about to cry.

"She'll be all right, Beau," Mick said, as much to himself as to the tiny dog. "She'll be all right."

He slammed the door shut and ran around to the driver's side. The sound of approaching sirens echoed in the distance, but he wasn't waiting. Before the engine had time to do little more than ignite, he slammed his foot down onto the accelerator and peeled away from the curb, barely conscious of the woman in the pink robe waving and yelling after him that she'd tell the police what had happened.

The emergency room was like a nightmare. There had been a pile-up on the freeway, a knifing on a streetcar; a mother was screaming that her daughter had accidentally put her hand through a window and was bleeding to death; several Mardi Gras celebrants had indulged in a little too much drink and ran their car into a telephone pole; and another had decided that since he had on a rooster costume, he could fly, but he'd found out differently after he jumped from the balcony of his second-story hotel room.

Mick stared at the door through which they'd taken B.J. He only cared about her.

"She'll be all right," he mumbled to himself. "She'll be all right." He absently nuzzled Beaujolais's ear. It was the first time he'd been to a hospital since Kyle . . . Mick pushed the thought away and focused his concentration on B.J. "She'll be all right," he said again.

A nurse moved to stand beside him. "I'm sorry, sir," she said coolly, "but you'll have to take the dog outside."

He didn't know what he'd do if the doctors came back out and said she was gone. It was his fault. The emptiness in his heart seemed to grow, its blackness spreading, threatening to devour him.

"Sir," the nurse snapped.

Mick spun around. "What? Is she . . . ?"

"You'll have to take the dog out," the nurse said sharply. She looked at Beaujolais as if he were some kind of slithering monster, and her long, pointed nose wrinkled. "Animals are not allowed in the hospital."

"Make an exception," Mick said. He turned to stare at the door again, willing one of the doctors to appear, to come and tell him B.J. was going to be all right.

"Sir, if you don't take the dog out," the nurse said, "I will have to call security and have you *both* removed."

Mick snatched his wallet from his pocket and turned to practically shove it in the woman's face. "I'm not going anywhere," he said with a growl, "and neither is the dog."

She pushed his badge from in front of her nose. "I don't care what you are," she said, "dogs are not—"

Mick's temper flared. "Lady, I don't care what your rules say."

The nurse cringed from him, her eyes wide with shock.

"This is official business, and neither I nor this dog is leaving until I know the lady in room Eight is going to be okay. Got it?"

She spun on her heel and stormed toward the reception desk. "Well, we'll just see about that," she muttered.

Mick turned to rivet his attention on the door again. He'd been a fool. He'd fallen for B.J. Just the thing he'd been afraid of, just the thing he'd known he should never do again, had vowed he would never do again. He might not have wanted to admit it earlier, might not have even realized it, but he knew it now, and that realization, along with his fear for her life, was eating him up inside.

He felt helpless, exactly the way he had the night Kyle had been taken away from him. Mick's mind filled with the memories he'd fought for years to keep at bay, and with them all the pain came rushing back. How could he go through that again? He'd never survive, never be able to endure that kind of pain again.

"Marshal."

He turned, recognizing the nurse's voice.

"I've called security," she said haughtily.

"Good for you." Mick turned away.

"They are coming to remove you."

He turned back to her, fury like none he'd ever known before burning within his chest, chasing away all reason. He glanced at her name badge. "Ms. Staples, have you ever had a visit from an IRS agent?" he asked caustically, his tone black and threatening. He glanced at the wedding ring on her left hand, knowing that what he was doing was highly unethical and not giving a damn. "Got a kid who gets in trouble, Ms. Staples? Maybe should spend a little time behind bars? Or maybe it's a husband who likes to drink a little too much on occasion? Or doesn't bother to pay his parking tickets?" Mick thrust his face into hers. "Believe me, lady, whatever little problem there is in your life, I can find it, and it won't be so little then."

The threat of what he'd do if he found the problem was clearly evident behind both his words and the black fire he knew was emanating from his eyes.

She glared at him. "You can't do that."

"No?" His eyes narrowed. "Watch me."

Two security officers suddenly appeared at the end of the hallway and walked toward them, one a burly middle-aged man, the other a wiry blond who looked more like he belonged in high school and working as a bag boy at the local grocery store than in one of the city's largest and busiest hospitals as a security officer.

Nurse Staples jumped when the burly officer stopped beside her. "You have trouble, Millie?" he said quietly, glowering at Mick.

She turned to him. "It was a . . . a misunderstanding, Joe. Sorry to get you up here for nothing."

He smiled. "Hey, trouble that's no trouble is the best kind, Millie." He glanced at Mick again, then looked at Beaujolais, still cradled in his arms, then turned his attention back to Nurse Staples. "But, you sure, Millie?"

"I'm sure," she said, and ushered them away.

"Nurse Staples," Mick said when she returned, shrugging away the guilt he felt at how he'd treated her. "One more thing?"

She stared at him.

"Could you see how Miss Poydras is doing? In room Eight?"

She spun on her heel and crashed through the swinging doors to room Eight without a backward glance.

Mick knew she'd probably like nothing better than to have her security officers strap him to a gurney and roll him onto the freeway, and if anything happened to B.J., he just might let Nurse Staples do that. But for now, he wanted to know what was going on, how B.J. was doing, that she was going to be alright.

The nurse slammed open the swinging doors and stalked toward him. "Miss Poydras should be out of emergency soon, and the doctor will talk to you then."

"Out?" Mick frowned. "As in released?" He couldn't believe that. It was too much to hope for.

"I'm not sure," she said, "that's all I'm at liberty to say." She turned away and started to walk toward the nurses' station.

"Nurse Staples," Mick called after her.

She stopped and turned around, fury and indignation pulling at her sharp features.

"Thank you. And I'm sorry for what I said earlier."

She lifted her chin defiantly. "You should be," she said, "but I knew you were bluffing all the time."

He smiled and turned back to wait for the doctor.

After a few more minutes the swinging doors opened and a young man in hospital greens walked toward him, removing his mask as he approached. He looked tired. Or maybe it was worried. Or sad. Mick's heart lurched and threatened to stop.

"Are you Mick?" the young doctor asked.

"Ah, yeah," Mick said, surprised. "Mick Gentry."

The doctor smiled and offered his hand. "I'm Doctor Kyle."

A lump formed in Mick's throat at hearing the man's name. "Kyle," he repeated numbly. Memories suddenly rained down on him and he struggled to push them away. This wasn't the time or the place.

The doctor nodded. "Miss Poydras has been asking for you."

That was another surprise. "She's okay then?"

"Miraculously, from what the nurse said you told her happened, her injuries are not serious. Frankly, I'm surprised, especially that her hip shows no fractures."

"Me too," Mick said.

The doctor looked at Beaujolais curiously, then focused his attention back on Mick. "She has a slight concussion, a lot of pretty bad bruises, and a sprained wrist. Other than that," he shrugged, "it looks like she'll be okay."

Mick nodded. "Can I see her?"

"Sure. They'll be taking her upstairs in a minute. I've given her a sedative though, so she might be pretty out of it, and she'll sleep for the next several hours. If she feels better, I'll consider releasing her later. You can go along to her room, though I'm not sure about your friend."

Mick smiled and rubbed Beau's head. "Oh, I think it will be all right, Doc. Nurse Staples will clear the way for the little guy."

"Nurse Staples?" the doctor said, clearly shocked. "Man, you must either have a real abundance of charm, Mr. Gentry, or a hell of a lot of pull around here."

"No, we just have an understanding," Mick said.

Five minutes later an orderly and a nurse wheeled B.J. past him. She looked so small on the gurney, he wanted to cry. Her face was nearly as white as the sheet, and her eyes remained closed. He thought about going to his hotel and trying to get some sleep, then coming back in a few hours, but decided against it. If she needed to sleep, fine. He would wait beside her bed until she woke up. He'd never get any sleep anyway, not until he was sure she was going to be okay, until he saw her open her eyes himself.

He followed them into the elevator, then down the long hallway of the third floor, and finally into a room. An old woman was sitting up in the room's other bed,

Tricks of the Trade

reading the newspaper, which she promptly set down on her lap when they entered.

"Ohhh, is she all right?" she said, watching them wheel B.J. past. Her old eyes were full of alarm. "Such a young little thing. What happened?"

"She was hit by a car," Mick said, as the nurse and orderly transferred B.J. to the bed.

"Oh, well it's good that you're here," the woman said. "A husband should be with his wife in times like this. And if you need anything, young man, my name is Mrs. Handlemier, and you just tell me." She smiled proudly. "The nurses like me."

He'd been about to deny that he was B.J.'s husband when he heard her moan and call out to him. Mick moved to the side of her bed. "I'm here, B.J.," he said, bending down close to her. "So is Beau," he whispered, holding the little dog so that he could sniff B.J.

She didn't open her eyes, but she smiled. "Take care of him, Mick. Please."

"We're not going anywhere," he said. "You sleep. We'll both be here when you wake up." He turned, saw a chair set against the far wall, and dragged it over beside the bed and settled himself down in it. Then he wondered if Beaujolais needed to go outside. The dog promptly curled into a ball in Mick's lap, the first time he'd seemed to relax since her accident, and closed his eyes.

"Well," he whispered, "I guess you just answered my question."

Five hours later the cellular phone in Mick's jacket pocket rang, waking him, Beaujolais, B.J., and Mrs. Handlemier. He bolted up from his slumped position in the chair, nearly sending Beaujolais flying to the floor but catching him just in time. Mick yanked the phone from his pocket and flipped it open. "Yeah?" he growled into the receiver, still trying to chase the sleep from his brain. His eyes focused on B.J. and a heavy weight seemed to suddenly lift from his heart as he noticed her looking back at him, her eyes clear. A bandage was taped to one temple and her hair was splayed about her shoulders in a tangle. At that moment he thought she was the most beautiful vision in the world.

"Gentry, that you?" Jarrett asked.

He sat up straighter and Beaujolais jumped down and began sniffing around the corners of the room.

"Yeah, it's me," Mick said. "What's up?"

"B.J. okay?"

He turned away from Beaujolais, realizing the dog hadn't been out in hours and was probably sniffing out a potential target for his relief. "Hold on," Mick said. Looking around quickly, he made do, grabbing the tie off of Mrs. Handlemier's robe, which lay on the foot of her bed, and looping it through Beaujolais's collar. He grabbed the phone as he waved to B.J. and hurried from the room toward the exit door at the end of the hall.

"Gentry, what in the hell are you doing?" Jarrett yelled. "I don't have all day, you know?"

Mick hurried down the stairs after Beau, pushed open the exterior exit door, and breathed a sigh of relief when the little dog darted straight for a nearby bush. "Jarrett," Mick said, lifting the phone to his ear, "sorry. The dog had to . . . oh, never mind. What's up?"

"I asked you how B.J. is."

"Fine. Concussion, bruises, and a sprained wrist. The doc wanted to keep her here for awhile for observation so I figured I should stay." He decided not to add the fact that the whole thing had been his fault.

"Good."

"So, what have you got?" Mick asked.

"Charbonneau's car. It's being towed into impound even as we speak. Found it out at the airport."

"Can I get into it?"

"After it's dusted, yeah."

"I'll meet you at your office in . . ." Mick looked at his watch. He had to go back up and see B.J., talk to her doctor, and make sure everything was really alright. Then he had to find somewhere to leave Beaujolais. He glanced down at the clothes he had on. His jeans were okay; his shirt, however, looked as if he'd slept in it—which he had. "I'll get there as soon as I can."

He turned to go back into the hospital and found that the exit door didn't open from the outside. "Oh great," he muttered. Now he'd have to go all the way around to the front, and most likely hassle with anyone and everyone he ran into about bringing the dog inside.

"Come on, Beau," he said. Mick slipped Mrs. Handlemier's robe tie from Beaujolais's collar and shoved it into the pocket of his jacket, then picked the dog up and cradled him against his chest and under his jacket. "Maybe no one will notice you."

He walked around the building and into the lobby.

The receptionist's brows soared as he entered. "I'm sorry sir, but you can't . . ."

Mick flashed his badge and kept on walking. "Sorry,

official business." Luckily for him the elevator doors were open. He dashed inside, jabbed the button for the third floor, and waved good-bye to the receptionist, who was on the phone, most likely to security.

Nurse Staples was still on duty, and standing at the nurses' station as he exited the elevator. She glanced at him, at Beaujolais, only half concealed under Mick's jacket, and shook her head. But Mick didn't fail to see the slight smile pulling at one corner of her lips. "We'll only be a minute, I promise," Mick said.

He walked into B.J.'s room, dropping Mrs. Handlemier's robe tie on her bed as he passed, and thanking the powers-that-be that the old lady wasn't in the room.

"Hi," B.J. said as Mick passed the curtain drawn between the two beds and came into view.

Beaujolais barked and began to struggle to get out of Mick's arms the minute he heard B.J.'s voice.

"Hi," Mick said. He suddenly wondered if she'd remember how angry she'd been at him just before she'd been hit by that car. Maybe she didn't want to see him. He felt a stab in his heart. He shouldn't have stayed, shouldn't have been there when she woke up. If he'd left her, it would have been over, the way it had to be. Mick cursed himself, knowing what he had to do and not wanting to do it. Beaujolais twisted, and Mick gave up his struggle to hold onto the dog. The animal flung himself onto the bed and bounced his way up to B.J., licking her face and burrowing himself a nest next to her shoulder.

ELEVEN

Mick watched Beaujolais greet B.J., but remained silent, not certain what to say, yet unable to make himself leave.

B.J. sighed and lay her head back against the mound of pillows behind her. With one hand resting on Beaujolais's back, she let her eyelids flutter closed.

Mick cursed the feelings that rose within him then. She looked frail, tired, so vulnerable that he suddenly and desperately wanted nothing more than to pull her into his arms and protect her from the world—something he knew from hard, cold experience that he couldn't do.

"Do you remember what happened?" Mick said, breaking the silence that was beginning to feel unbearable. His voice sounded brittle, strained, and he cursed that too.

B.J.'s brow furrowed into a frown. Did she remember what happened? She forced herself to try, in spite of the dull ache that seemed to fill her head and culminate in a steady throbbing at her left temple. Raising a hand, she tentatively touched the bandage on her head with trembling fingers, as if that could somehow ease the pain. "A black car," she said finally, her voice little more than a whisper. "I mean . . . I think it was black. Dark."

"Do you remember the make?" Mick asked, his cop mode instinctively kicking in. Make—model—color. He had the color, but he needed more. Jarrett had told him the old lady at the scene, the one who'd helped him, had said it was black, too, but that's all she had seen.

B.J.'s frown deepened at his question.

Mick watched her eyes close, as if she were trying to force her memory to cooperate, and felt like cutting out his tongue for questioning her.

But it was standard procedure, his cop side reminded him. Get the details while they're fresh in the victim's mind.

He tried to shrug the sensible thought away. This was B.J. he was badgering with questions, B.J. who had almost been killed. She was the woman he had made love to only a few hours earlier, not some nameless victim.

She tried to clear the blur of thoughts and images crowding her mind. She'd been angry. The intensity of the feeling began to come back to her. She'd been angry just before it had happened. But why? She opened her eyes and looked up at Mick, about to ask him if he knew, when it suddenly all came flooding back. She'd been angry with him because he'd used her. She'd also been angry that she'd allowed herself to be used. B.J. pushed that thought away as a sharp response to him formed in her mind. The words were about to burst forth from her lips when she also remembered something else. *"Don't leave me, B.J."*

The anger suddenly drained away as swiftly and as completely as it had come to her. But not the hurt. B.J. tried to smile, found that the effort sent pain searing through her temple, and let it go. She'd probably misinterpreted his words anyway. He'd most likely meant nothing more than that she shouldn't die, that he needed her to help him with his case, to tell him who'd hit her, because he thought it had something to do with this Charbonneau/Townsend thing. That's all, nothing more, nothing personal. "No," she whispered finally, as he watched her. "Big and black, that's all I remember. It came out of nowhere, seemed to aim straight for me."

"You didn't see anyone? Recognize the driver? Even get a glimpse of him?" He knew he shouldn't push her, but this was the time for her to think about it, before the images faded. Someone had tried to kill her. As far as he was concerned, she was still in danger.

"I remember Beaujolais stopping at the curb and barking," B.J. said finally, "but I ignored him. Then I turned and yelled at him. That's when I caught a glimpse of the car." She also remembered that her last conscious thought after being hit had been about Mick. In spite of her anger at him, in spite of the fact that he'd made her feel cheap and easy, her last thought before losing consciousness had been a wish that she could see his face just one more time. Well, that prayer had been answered a little too generously, she thought now. Too bad she hadn't asked for a million dollars instead. A Ferrari, a villa in Italy, and maybe a few hundred thousand stocks in some huge conglomerate or other. She inhaled deeply and went on. "I remember hearing you call my name."

Mick touched her hand gently, wanting to hold it, to pull her into his arms and assure himself by touching her, feeling her warm and vibrant against him, that she was really all right. But he refrained, holding himself stiffly, not certain if his embrace was welcome, and remembering that she'd been walking away from him at the time of the accident, which had been exactly what he'd wanted.

But not anymore, a voice in the back of his mind screamed.

He ignored it. Nothing had really changed in that respect. It was still better that this thing that had erupted between them be stopped, the feelings repressed. She had her life and he had his. They didn't mesh. And she didn't need a man carrying around as much emotional baggage as he had on his back anyway. No woman did. And he certainly didn't need to accumulate any more, or cause another woman the kind of pain he was more than capable of inflicting.

"I got a call from Jarrett a few minutes ago," he said, then wished he hadn't. The case was the last thing she needed to be concerned with at the moment. This entire thing was his fault. He should never have gone to her office, never have gotten her involved. Mick cursed beneath his breath.

"Excuse me?" B.J. said, looking at him questioningly.

He looked up sharply, not having been aware he'd even spoken aloud. Never again, he promised himself, even as his gaze moved hungrily over her. No matter what happened on a case in the future, he would pursue things on his own, alone, the way he usually did. And, if it happened that he did need to use someone else, he would keep his distance, the way he should have done with B.J.

"They found Charbonneau's car at the airport," he said finally, figuring to tell her what he knew and then leave quickly. "It's in impound now being dusted for prints. Seems a little weird that it wasn't there the first time they looked, but . . ." he shrugged. "Things happen. At least it's not in the swamp—which leaves one to wonder how, if his car was at the airport, the body in the morgue that they found out at the Charbonneau cabin could be Charbonneau, doesn't it?" An insolent chuckle rumbled from his throat. "Especially since you seem so certain Mr. Charbonneau committed suicide. But," he shrugged, "weirder things have happened, I guess."

Maybe to you, B.J. wanted to say.

"Anyway, I'm going to go down and take a look at it."

"I want to go," she said, and tried to push herself up from the pillows. The strain of the effort showed in the frown that immediately drew at her brow and the dark shadow that swept into her eyes.

"The doctor says you have a concussion," Mick barked, his tone hard and commanding. He didn't want her to come, not only because she was hurt, but because he didn't trust himself to keep it all business between them anymore, didn't trust himself to walk away from her the way he knew he had to do. "I'll let you know if I find anything." A feeling of guilt settled over him at the lie. He had no intention of coming back. Jarrett could fill her in if they found any leads from their examination of the car, as well as any other developments of the case that came up while she was recuperating. B.J. was going to be okay, and that's all Mick had needed to know. Now he could leave.

"I want to go," B.J. said again, more sternly this time, more determined. She threw aside the bedsheet and, grimacing as she moved, swung her legs over the side of the bed. "It could be that someone else drove that car to the airport, you know. Would you get my clothes?"

"No."

"Fine, then I'll get them myself." She pushed herself off the bed. "Should know better than to ask a man to do something for me anyway. Especially a cop." Her feet touched the floor, and as soon as she put her weight on them, her knees buckled.

Mick swooped forth and caught her in his arms. "Dammit, B.J.," he said, as much because of her foolish act as because of the desire that swept through him the moment his arms went around her and he felt her body pressed to his.

"Well, I did ask you to get my clothes for me," she replied sharply, twisting out of his arms while holding to the bed. Her face flushed as she rejected the need to stay within the safe harbor of his embrace. He'd only wanted to bed her, and she'd do well to remember that.

"Oh, all right," he groused, "but don't expect me to catch you every time you start to faint." He retrieved her clothes from the small hospital closet. "And don't expect me to help you sign yourself out of this hospital."

"I wasn't going to faint," she said, bristling, as she snatched her clothes from his outstretched hand. "And I

Tricks of the Trade

don't need you to help me sign out of this place, or do anything else for that matter."

Mick felt as if someone had just kicked him in the gut, and at that moment he knew, undeniably, just how deep his feelings for B.J. had grown, and how profoundly she'd penetrated his defenses, his heart. "Oh, really?" was all he could manage.

"Yes, really," B.J. said. She turned toward the small bathroom, intending to change her clothes. "In fact, I'll drive myself over to impound, so you don't even have to wait for me." Her legs were still wobbly, and she felt weak as hell, but she was not going to let him see that. She'd always stood on her own two feet, literally and figuratively, and she would do it now. She didn't need him. And she certainly didn't want him.

"Your car isn't here," Mick reminded her. Why didn't he just walk away? He cursed himself. What the hell did he want? But the moment he had the thought, he knew it didn't matter what he wanted. Leaving, walking away from her before this thing between them got any more out of hand than it already had, was what he had to do. It was for the best, for both of them.

B.J. was about to retort that she'd take a taxi when she realized that she didn't have her bag, and that she'd been so angry when she'd stormed out of the condo that she hadn't grabbed her wallet, as she always did when she jogged, which meant she didn't have any money to pay for a cab. She glared at Mick, hating to give in to him, and knowing she had no choice if she wanted to get to impound now. "Fine, I'll go with you, since you're going there anyway, and send you a check for gas later."

"The Fed pays for my gas," Mick quipped.

"Fine. Then I'll mail them a check."

"Fine." *Am I going to go through the rest of my life wanting to strangle her?*

The thought struck him from out of nowhere, and Mick nearly reeled. He backed up to the wall and leaned against it, momentarily needing its support, its stability. What in hell was he thinking? There was no "rest of his life" with her or any other woman. In fact, if he had his way, after this little sojourn to impound, he wouldn't even see her again.

"Okay, I'm ready," B.J. said minutes later, breaking into his thoughts as she tossed the hospital gown onto the bed.

Ten minutes after that they were seated in his car and pulling out of the hospital parking lot, Doctor Kyle's words of caution to B.J. about taking it easy having fallen on deaf ears, as Mick had known they would.

She sat with her arms crossed over her breasts and stared straight ahead. Okay, she told herself for the hundredth time in the last hour, she'd made a fool of herself, let him into her bed and into her heart, but that was over. *"Don't leave me, B.J."* Hah! she thought. He'd probably meant, "don't leave me B.J. without telling me if it was Carl Townsend driving the car that hit you." So, from now on it was strictly business. "Well," she said, her tone cool and sharp, "we're obviously making progress with this thing."

"They found Charbonneau's car, B.J.," Mick said, "not him. And maybe nothing else."

"I wasn't referring to Charbonneau's car," B.J. said

Tricks of the Trade

testily. "I was referring to the fact that someone tried to kill me."

"Or was merely a very bad driver." That was a preferable thought.

"Yeah, right," she said with a sneer. "Considering how wide the street is in front of my place, I doubt that."

He felt like growling. When the woman was right, she was right. "Got any other enemies? Anyone from a previous case who'd like to see you floating on a cloud and strumming your harp?"

"Shoveling coal in hell is more likely," she grumbled, "but he's in the state pen."

"I'm not playing bodyguard," Mick said. He sounded cold and mean, and that's exactly how he wanted to sound. Keep her at a distance, he kept telling himself, for her sake if not your own.

"Thank you," B.J. said. "But I didn't ask you to. We're both professionals. I can take care of myself, and you can take care of yourself."

He didn't miss the hurt in her tone and could have kicked himself in the rear for causing it. But he knew now that it was less hurt than she'd feel if he allowed this thing between them to go on.

Mick sat in one of the chairs in front of Jarrett's desk and stared at the lab's report on Theodore Charbonneau's car. "Son of a. . . ." He tossed the report onto Jarrett's desk. "We've got Townsend's prints, Evie Strindel's prints, and an unidentified set of prints in Charbonneau's car that are most likely Charbonneau's.

That proves the two men were connected. But how? And which one is it lying in the morgue?" He was getting frustrated as hell, and the feeling didn't totally stem from the case. He tried to keep his gaze averted from B.J.

"You're probably right," Jarrett said, "about those being Charbonneau's prints, but we can't be certain 'til they're identified, and right now it doesn't look like the man was ever printed, so identifying them might not happen."

"Which leaves us absolutely nowhere," Mick snapped.

"Townsend could have hijacked Theodore and Evie and made them drive him somewhere," B.J. said. She knew that was a weak offering, but she had this insane urge to argue against anything and everything Mick said about Theodore Charbonneau. She wanted him to be the body in the morgue, a man who'd died in an accidental fire, and her case to be involved only with finding the dog he'd taken to the cabin with him that day.

But she couldn't help but admit to herself that the likelihood of that was pretty slim now. She knew Mick was right, that somehow Charbonneau and Carl Townsend were connected, involved in something together, but she wasn't going to admit that to him. Not until she had to.

And where was ChiChi?

"Right," Mick said, glancing at her, then quickly looking away. "Townsend kidnapped them, then killed Charbonneau and set him and the cabin on fire, let Evie go, and left the car at the airport a couple of weeks later, boarded a plane for San Francisco, then came back here

Tricks of the Trade

and disappeared again." He shrugged mockingly. "Sounds real reasonable."

"As you've said," B.J. countered coldly, "things happen."

He looked at her, about to bark out another snappish retort, but cut off the words before they could leave his mouth. She looked exhausted. There were dark circles under her eyes, and no spark to her tone. Her shoulders sagged uncharacteristically. She looked weary and worn and his snapping probably wasn't helping any.

Mick rose abruptly. "I'm taking you home."

B.J. stiffened against his authoritative manner. "I'll take a cab."

"On what?" Mick demanded.

She turned to Jarrett. "Would you loan me twenty dollars until tomorrow?"

"Sure." Jarrett started to reach for his wallet.

"I said I'd take you home," Mick said again. "Someone tried to kill you, and Jarrett can't offer round-the-clock protection in case it happens again."

"Good," B.J. said. "I'll take care of myself."

"The way you did last time?" Mick challenged. He didn't know why he was insisting on this. As he'd said earlier, he wasn't her bodyguard. But he couldn't let go, because if something happened to her that he could have prevented if he'd been there to do it, he'd never forgive himself, never be able to live with himself again.

"I need to stop by the office," B.J. said to Jarrett, holding her hand out for the money she'd requested. "I'll check in with you later."

"Your secretary can handle the office," Mick said. "I've already talked to her."

B.J. spun around and stared at him, surprised and indignant. "You talked to Alice? When?" she demanded, not sounding at all grateful.

"Earlier. Now come on." He held out his hand. Their raised voices had drawn the attention of the other detectives in the room. Mick didn't like scenes, didn't like being the center of attention, but he wasn't going to let B.J. leave alone. Someone had tried to kill her and, for all he knew, might try again. He would just have to keep his emotions in check and under control. His body too. This would make it that much harder to leave her later, he knew. But he had no choice.

"You know, Marshal, you really are a—"

"Yeah, I know," Mick said, cutting her off. He looked back at Jarrett as B.J. rose. "Hold on a second, B.J." Grabbing Jarrett's phone, he dialed his office.

"If you're making a long distance call, Gentry," Jarrett said, "you'd best be doing it on your own dime. Especially from my phone."

Mick punched in his ID code and his secretary's phone rang. "No problem," he mouthed to Jarrett. "Tina, I need you to do something. You checked into that dead cousin of Townsend's already. Now I need a picture of the cousin, anything on what his financial status was like when he died, any girlfriends, friends, job associates, other relatives, anything. See if the guys in Special Detail can figure a way he could have faked his own death. If so, did he have any resources stashed away, where would he have gone, what would he have done for cash? And check

Tricks of the Trade

the record for his fingerprints, under any alias. Jarrett will send you the prints we have for comparison; fax us back everything you get." Mick hung up and glanced at an obviously surprised Jarrett. "Thanks." He turned to B.J. "Let's go."

"Not until you explain what that was all about," she said, sitting back down on the corner of Jarrett's desk and crossing her arms. A gleam of stubbornness shone from her eyes. Mick cursed it, then realized it was better than the dullness that had been there a few seconds before.

"Yeah, I wouldn't mind an explanation myself," Jarrett said.

Mick sighed. He should have known better than to make that phone call in front of them, especially in front of B.J., but he'd been mulling over a theory for the past several hours, and he'd needed to move on it.

He settled into the chair before Jarrett's desk, a long sigh rushing from his lips as he did. "Okay, I've been thinking." He paused, sliding a hand through his hair, and looked up at B.J., waiting for some wise remark. When none came, he continued, though admittedly somewhat surprised by her silence. "Carl had a cousin, Jason Townsend. They were almost the same age, about a year apart I think, but they looked alike, a lot alike, even had the same build. Their fathers were identical twins. Anyway, we always figured Jason was the set-up man for the bank jobs, but when we caught Jason, Carl, and their buddy Tom, none would rat on the other, so they were all set up with separate trials. Jason made bail. Before his trial date came up, he was dead. Mangled beyond recognition in a car wreck that turned into an inferno."

"You told me that already," B.J. said. "About Jason," she added.

"Yeah, I know." Mick nodded. "But it's been bothering me." He suddenly sat forward, an intense look in his eyes. "I mean, look at this thing. Jason supposedly died in a fire. His body was unidentifiable, but there were things at the scene that said it was him. His false teeth had been thrown clear of the wreck, and his wallet was found between the car's seats, charred, but still intact. Everyone, including me, wanted to believe it was Jason Townsend. All the evidence said it was, so we accepted it, in spite of the fact that a damned wallet had survived a fire that was hot enough to burn the guy's body beyond recognition."

"Air pocket," B.J. said, playing the devil's advocate.

"Maybe. But keep looking," Mick countered. "Now we've got Charbonneau, same scenario: dead in a fire, his body unidentifiable, but everyone assumes it's Charbonneau because of where it was found—at the family cabin—and because the remains fit the general characteristics of Charbonneau. Should be case closed," Mick said. He shrugged. "The dead man is Theodore Charbonneau."

"That's what I've been saying," B.J. said.

Mick smiled. "Yes, but you've left out Carl Townsend."

"You've never proven the two men even knew each other."

"No, but I've proven they came in contact. Remember," he looked at Jarrett, "Townsend used Charbonneau's credit card in San Francisco, then he came to New Orleans, Charbonneau's home. Shortly thereafter, both men disappeared. Then we discover the car with Townsend's prints."

Mick sat back and smiled, but B.J. could find no trace of smugness in the gesture. She wished she could, so she'd have a reason for disliking him other than the fact that he just plain infuriated her and made her blood boil. It galled her to think that he could get to her like that.

"I'd say Mick's right, there's a definite connection, and it's pretty obvious that only one of them is still alive," Jarrett said.

"Well, I still say you could be wrong."

"And it's pretty coincidental both Townsends had false teeth. Are you sure Carl does?"

"Yes. They were in some kind of accident together as teenagers, had most of their teeth knocked out."

"You still could be wrong," B.J. said, stubbornly hanging onto that thought, "but if you aren't, that would mean . . ."

Mick smiled up at her. "That would mean Theodore Charbonneau really was, or is, Jason Townsend."

"And either he murdered Carl," Jarrett said, "or Carl murdered him."

"If it's murder," B.J. said, still resistant to the idea.

TWELVE

"What he says makes sense," Jarrett said. He looked at B.J. as if he expected her to argue the point.

She picked up Beaujolais, who had been napping next to Jarrett's desk, and hugged him close, feeling the need suddenly, amidst all this talk of death and only hours after her own close call, to reassure herself that she was still alive. "But we haven't really proven anything yet."

Jarrett reached for the phone on his desk, punched a number, and told whomever answered to do a background check on Lillian Charbonneau and her husband Theodore. "And not that society page garbage they hand out," he said. "I want everything on them since they were born, and before that if possible."

She turned to Mick. "If you're right, this is going to blow the society types around here right out of the water, you know?" Her remark made him chuckle. "So, which one do you think is in the morgue—Carl or Jason?"

Mick shrugged. "I don't know."

Tricks of the Trade

B.J. hadn't expected that response and merely stared at him. He turned to Jarrett. "While we're waiting on hearing from my secretary, I'm going to take B.J. home. She's bushed. Call me if Tina faxes you anything before I get back." He glanced at B.J., fully expecting her to object.

She thought about it, not liking someone else to decide what she was going to do, or where she was going to go, but she was suddenly just too tired.

When she didn't argue, Mick leaned over Jarrett's desk and wrote something on his scratch pad. "That's my cellular number." He straightened. "And get ahold of the coroner and have him do another autopsy on our body."

Jarrett, who'd been lazing back in his chair, bolted upright. "What for?"

"When they brought the body in it seemed pretty evident who it was and what happened to him, right?"

Jarrett nodded.

"That's what for. They only did a preliminary-type autopsy," Mick said. "They probably didn't look for anything that shouldn't be there, like a knife wound, a bullet hole, a broken larynx. You get the picture."

"Yeah," Jarrett said. He reached for the phone.

B.J. got a sudden spurt of energy. "You don't think he died in the fire?"

"No. I think the fire was set to cover up the real way he died."

"Could be hard to prove," Jarrett said over the receiver after he punched in the number. "That body isn't in too good a condition."

"I know." Mick turned to B.J. "Ready to go?"

She hesitated. Mentally she wanted to sit and wait for Mick's secretary to call back, and the coroner to come back with results of a second autopsy. Physically she wanted nothing more than to lie down and go to sleep. *Preferably in Mick's arms.* The thought came at her out of nowhere, and she tried to shove it back there. If she ever ended up in his arms again, it would only be because hell had frozen over.

B.J. glanced around the precinct room. How many people had he left her phone number with, "just in case he was needed"? The thought stoked her anger. He'd given it out *before* he'd taken her home, *before* she'd invited him in, *before* they'd made love. Which meant he'd assumed beforehand that he'd be staying at her place. Her hands clenched into fists. *That's* what infuriated her. *That's* what made her feel like a first-class fool. And if there was anything B.J. didn't like, it was feeling like a fool.

She wanted to tell him she'd find her own way home, in her own time, when she realized several people were watching her, probably waiting to see if she'd make a scene. She stiffened. "Yes," she said softly and rose. Beaujolais jumped to the floor and headed toward the door. "Let's go."

B.J. fumbled with the door key. Why was she having such a hard time getting it into the lock?

Mick reached over and took it from her hand, then gently moved her out of the way. A second later he shoved the door open.

Tricks of the Trade

Beaujolais entered and B.J. followed, then turned quickly, trying to block him from following her into the condo, but she was too late.

"You lie down," Mick said, taking hold of her shoulders and urging her toward her bedroom. "Undress and settle in, I'll feed the dog and make you some soup."

"I hate soup," B.J. said.

"Fine. I'll make you something else. Go." He gave her a slight push toward the bedroom door. She glanced over her shoulder and saw him head for the kitchen.

B.J. changed into pale blue jogging pants and sweatshirt, ran a brush through her hair, and tied it at her nape with a ribbon. Comfortable but far from sexy, which is exactly what she wanted to be. She walked back into the living room and sat on the sofa.

"I thought I told you to get into bed," Mick said, looking at her over the counter that separated kitchen from living room. The blue of her sweatshirt brought out the blue of her eyes. Though the outfit was rather a baggy one, he had no problem discerning the lines of her body, and that was something he could most definitely do without.

"You said undress and settle in," B.J. countered. "That's what I've done."

He sighed in exasperation. "Do you ever cooperate with anyone?"

"No," she said, remembering the last time he'd been in her apartment. She'd cooperated with him then and lost a great big chunk of her heart. "It only gets me into trouble."

Mick walked into the living room carrying a plate. "Eat up," he said, "then go to bed and get some rest."

B.J. stared at the concoction steaming on the plate. She'd never seen anything like it and wasn't sure she wanted to eat it. She tried to think of a delicate way to ask him what it was, but the question must have been clear on her face.

"My mother used to give this to me whenever I was sick," Mick said. "Now, when I don't feel good, it's all I want to eat." He shrugged and smiled. "Brainwashed, I guess."

B.J. nodded, but still made no move to accept the plate.

"Mushroom soup, a can of drained tuna, mixed, heated, and poured over bread," Mick said. "It's good. Taste it." He shoved the plate toward her.

B.J. took it, and a bite of the concoction. Surprised, she looked up at him and smiled. But then, there were a lot of things about Mick Gentry that had surprised her. He was a romantic. Protective of injured women and small dogs. And he was a nurse and cook. "It is good."

"Of course it is," he said. "Why do you think my mother gave it to me?"

"You're not having any?"

"Nope. Like I said, I eat it when I don't feel good, but right now I feel fine." Except that his pants were too tight again, his blood pressure felt as if it were soaring, and he wanted her so badly, he could scream.

"You don't have to stay, you know?"

"I know." But he didn't want to leave. Mick tried to tell himself it was because he was afraid someone might come after her again, if she were left alone. But he knew that wasn't the real reason.

B.J. sat back against the couch. Beaujolais jumped up and curled into a ball next to her, leaning into her thigh. "That really was good."

"I'll tell my mother," Mick said. He rose and took her plate. "Now go to bed."

She didn't move.

"I'll be out here. If you need anything, call me. I'll sleep on the couch."

Why did she feel suddenly disappointed? The image of his arms around her flashed through her mind, and she stiffened against it. Physical desire, that's all it was, she told herself. Nothing more. "You don't have to stay," she said again.

"I know."

Her gaze met his, and for a few seconds B.J. forgot that she was angry at him, wanted nothing more than to reach out to him, to feel his warmth and strength surround her.

"Go to bed, B.J.," Mick said, fighting against the desire to pull her into his arms. There were only two things he could offer her: pain and safety. He'd already hurt her enough. Now he would do everything he could to make certain no one else hurt her.

She rose. "There are extra sheets and blankets in the hall closet," B.J. said softly. She didn't know why she wasn't ordering him to leave, she only knew she was glad he was staying.

Three hours later Mick's cellular phone rang. He flipped it open. "Gentry," he said into the receiver.

"Mick, this is Jarrett. Your fax came in, and I've got a few things to go with it. I think you'd better come down here."

"Can't it wait until morning, Jarrett?" Mick stared into the darkness. "B.J.'s asleep."

"You really want it to?"

"I'm not asleep anymore," B.J. said, walking into the room, "so whatever it is, it doesn't have to wait."

Mick turned, realizing the phone's ring must have woken her up. He also realized that arguing with her wouldn't do him any good. "You can't stay here alone," he said.

"I hadn't planned to. I'm going with you."

"We'll be down in about thirty," he said to the detective, then clicked off.

"What did he find?" B.J. asked.

Mick shook his head. "He didn't say, just that he thought I should come down right away."

She nodded. "I'll be ready in five minutes."

It took ten, but he didn't care. When she walked back into the living room he studied her critically and, to his chagrin, hungrily. Everything about her, from the way she looked to the way she moved, fueled his desires. "Are you sure you feel up to going out?" His voice sounded raspy, and he paused to clear his throat. "You haven't had much sleep." Mick silently pleaded for strength as two thoughts swept through his mind: He needed to leave her, and he needed to love her.

"I've had more sleep than you," B.J. said.

"I don't sleep much." Anymore, he added silently.

Jarrett was smiling smugly as they approached his desk.

"You look like the cat who caught the mouse," B.J. said. She'd meant to sound cheerfully flippant. Instead she heard herself sound hard and sarcastic. Probably because her head was throbbing, she told herself, and most likely because as she'd lain on her bed, and Mick had lain on her couch, the two of them separated by only a thin wall, she'd spent more time yearning to be in his arms, to feel his body pressed to hers, taste the passion of his lips and the caress of his hands, than she had sleeping.

"Maybe I am," Jarrett shot back.

"What's up?" Mick asked. He was in a bad mood and taking it out on Jarrett, and he didn't care. This case was taking too long to wrap up, and if his gut instinct was right, which it usually was, Carl Townsend was dead anyway. But that wasn't what was firing his temper and he knew it. He'd just spent several hours lying on a couch, separated from B.J. by merely a wall and his own sense of right and wrong, and all the while he'd ached to make love to her so badly, he'd sworn dying couldn't be any worse.

"Your secretary sent several more faxes since we talked," Jarrett said, "and the autopsy report came back from the coroner. You were right, the guy in the morgue didn't die because of the fire—he was already dead."

B.J. bit on her bottom lip, not certain whether she was pleased or dismayed at this new bit of information. She'd been hired to find a dog, and was now on the trail of a murderer. She glanced at Mick. This was what she'd opened her agency to do, the kind of case she had always wanted to work, but she would have been better off, professionally and personally, if it hadn't brought Mick Gentry into her life along with it.

"Okay, Jarrett," Mick said, "don't keep us hanging. What killed him?"

"A bullet to the head."

"A bullet?" B.J. exclaimed. Her mouth dropped open in surprise. "But how? I mean, why didn't the coroner find that on the initial autopsy? I'd think that was pretty obvious, even if the guy was toasted."

"Well, first," Jarrett said, "he wasn't looking for it, and second, it went through the roof of the guy's mouth and lodged in his brain."

B.J. cringed. "Lodged in his brain?"

"Yeah, along with a piece of plastic from his missing dentures."

"Murder," Mick said.

"Yep, murder," Jarrett agreed. "Unless he committed suicide, but that theory doesn't quite fly."

"Why?" B.J. looked from one man to the other.

"Because," Mick said, explaining before Jarrett could, "there was no gun found at the scene of the crime, and even if somehow it landed in the swamp, who started the fire? And who took the guy's teeth, and left Charbonneau's car at the airport?"

"There's more," Jarrett said. "Those unidentified prints we found in Charbonneau's car."

"Jason's," Mick said.

"Yep. Your secretary faxed us a report from Interpol.

Looks like Jason took a little trip to France after he supposedly 'died' in that car accident, but he got himself into a little trouble there, before he decided he'd better start using an alias. His prints and picture weren't in the regular file because he was arrested but never prosecuted. That's why it took awhile to locate them." He took a folder from his desk and tossed it toward Mick and B.J. "And, our guy Jason had himself a little plastic surgery while he was in Paris."

B.J. stared down at a picture of a man who looked exactly like the man holding ChiChi in the photo Lillian Charbonneau had given her.

"I had a guy go out to the Charbonneau place and get a few personal items of Theodore Charbonneau's from the widow to compare prints with, and guess what?"

"They match," Mick said.

"Sure do. And we found out that she met Theodore in Paris." He slid a copy of a French newspaper's society column, along with one from New Orleans, across the desk. Both had a picture of Lillian and Theodore Charbonneau on their wedding day in Paris.

"Hello, Jason," Mick said.

B.J. picked up one of the papers and stared at the picture. "This is impossible. You're saying Lillian Charbonneau, a member of one of New Orleans's most prominent families, married a bank robber."

Mick smiled. "Things happen."

She tossed the paper back onto Jarrett's desk. "Okay, so we have a murderer to catch. Which one? And how?"

"Jarrett has a murderer to catch," Mick said. "I have

an escaped con to catch, if he's still alive, and you have a dog to find."

"Very funny," B.J. snapped, not at all amused. "The cases have all turned into one, as you have been insisting all along, so don't try to push me out now, Gentry."

Jarrett shoved his chair away from his desk and stood. "You know, I have a feeling something's going on here that has nothing to do with this case, so if you'll excuse me, I have an APB to check on, and I think I'll get some coffee." He walked away.

"I wasn't trying to push you out," Mick said, his tone hard and cold. "I was merely putting things into perspective."

"Oh, and I have things totally out of perspective, is that what you're saying?"

"I'm saying," Mick said with a growl, "that someone tried to kill you, and it's my fault for involving you in this thing in the first place."

Her flash of temper started to subside, until he continued.

"You have a concussion, B.J., and if you weren't so stubborn you'd be in bed resting like the doctor wanted, not traipsing around looking for a murderer, which is not what you were hired to do anyway."

"So you're saying that when a case gets difficult, you don't think I'm qualified or capable to handle it?"

"I didn't say that," Mick said, on the verge of losing all control over his temper now. "Stop putting words into my mouth."

"I don't have to put words into your mouth, Marshal," B.J. snapped back. "You have enough thoughtless ones tumbling out on your own."

Cops protected cops. If he strangled her now, he'd probably get away with it. Except that to strangle her he'd have to touch her, and if he touched her, the desire that was turning his aching loins into a blazing inferno would overpower him and he'd probably throw her to the floor and make love to her right there in front of everyone.

B.J. glanced around. Everyone was staring while trying to look as if they weren't. "Great," she said under her breath, "now look what you've done." She spun and walked toward the door.

She inhaled deeply, then exhaled slowly, forcing herself to calm down. The world spun for just a second and her head throbbed. B.J. pressed a hand to the wall beside her and leaned into it. Jumping down Mick's throat had been stupid. It wasn't his fault. He was a man, and getting a woman into bed was always the first thing on any man's mind. So he'd merely been doing what came naturally. She'd been the fool. Again. But at least this time she hadn't let it go on, hadn't fooled herself into thinking she was in love with him and gotten engaged for the fourth time.

Her mother hadn't been thrilled at any of the other prospects she'd chosen for matrimony. A cop would have sent her reeling over the edge.

Mick came out of the police station. He brushed past her and walked toward his car.

"I'm going to drive out to ask Mrs. Charbonneau a few questions," Mick said. "Want to go?" He held open the passenger door for her. He hadn't wanted to take her along, but he didn't want her home alone, or worse, running around the city alone. Someone had already tried to kill her once.

B.J. looked up at him, surprised by the offer. "Yes," she said, and climbed into the car. There was no reason they couldn't work together. She could remain professional.

"If you're right," B.J. said, as they drove toward the Charbonneau estate, "how did Carl know the name Jason was using, or that Jason was even alive and in San Francisco?"

Mick shrugged. "I figure someone who knew them both saw Jason and told Carl. It's the only explanation."

"But why, ah, would one of them kill the other?"

"Maybe Jason killed Carl to keep from giving him his share of the bank money. It was never recovered. Or, maybe Carl killed Jason after getting it, or because Jason wouldn't give it to him."

"But Carl could have blackmailed Jason for more, I mean, because Jason wouldn't have wanted Lillian to find out about his past. So why kill him?"

"Maybe he didn't."

He pulled the car into the circular drive of the Charbonneau estate, then looked at B.J. "You okay?"

There were faint dark shadows under her eyes and he knew, by the way she kept touching her temple every few seconds, that she had a headache.

B.J. forced a smile. "I'm fine."

They walked up the path toward the entry door.

"Doesn't seem like anyone's here," B.J. said.

"Her car was in the garage."

A few minutes later, after no one answered their knock, Mick began walking down the long gallery looking into windows. "Empty," he said, walking back to where B.J. still stood in front of the entry door. "Come on." He steered her toward the back door, where he pulled a small leather pouch from his jacket pocket and slipped a thin silver rod into the door's lock.

B.J. frowned. "What are you doing?"

"Getting in. Something's wrong."

"But . . . that's . . . illegal."

He pushed open the door, then coughed and stepped back, pulling her with him. "And that's gas."

B.J. waved at the suffocating fumes that wafted out at them.

Shoving his cellular phone into B.J.'s hand, Mick pulled the front of his shirt from his jeans. "Call the fire department," he yelled, then pulled the shirtfront up over his mouth and nose and dashed into the house.

"Mick," B.J. yelled after him, suddenly terrified. She quickly dialed 911 and gave the Charbonneau address. B.J. pulled her own shirt over her face and stepped into the kitchen. "Mick?"

No answer.

Her heart thudded madly. "Mick, answer me," she pleaded.

After checking the living and dining rooms, Mick had run upstairs. The gas fumes weren't as strong upstairs yet, but they were there, and Mrs. Charbonneau was lying unconscious on the floor of her bedroom. Kicking open the room's French doors, Mick dragged her onto the second story gallery, then hefted her into his arms as he spotted a stairway leading to the ground, and hurried toward it. If the damned house blew, he didn't want to be in it.

Collapsing on the lawn, Mick knelt over Lillian and felt her neck for a pulse. It was strong. He turned to tell B.J. "She's going to . . ." The words stuck in his throat. Mick jumped up and looked around. "B.J." He coughed, his voice hoarse. "B.J.?" he called again, louder this time. "B.J.?" He ran toward the open back door and into the house.

B.J. turned the last knob on the stove and ran for the kitchen door. She was almost to it when she collided with someone running toward her. The air flew from her lungs along with a soft shriek of surprise.

"B.J.," Mick said. Grabbing her arm, he whirled about and raced from the house, coughing as he fell to his knees on the lawn. Beside him B.J. lay on her back, gasping for breath.

"Damn," Mick whispered, then pulled B.J. into his arms and crushed her against his chest. She could have been killed. Gone, forever, like Kyle. He felt his heart twist savagely, felt the ache of loss fill every cell in his body. Gripping her upper arms, he held her away from him. "What's the matter with you?" he demanded harshly, anger at her, at himself, at the situation, overwhelming him. "You could have been killed."

The wail of sirens suddenly broke the silence of their surroundings.

Mrs. Charbonneau began to cough, then sat up. "Oh, my heavens," she said, grabbing her head and swaying.

Tricks of the Trade

Breaking away from Mick, B.J. turned toward the older woman.

Mick moved to Lillian Charbonneau's side. "What happened?"

She shook her head and looked up at him, her gaze darting from Mick to B.J. and back to Mick. "I . . . it's the servants' day off and—" She shook her head again, then cringed in pain.

"Easy, Mrs. Charbonneau," B.J. said. "What happened?"

"I was reading, downstairs, and I fell asleep. When I woke up I decided to change clothes and went upstairs, and he hit me."

"He hit you," B.J. repeated. "Who?"

Mrs. Charbonneau's eyes grew large. "Theodore."

"Your husband?" Mick asked.

"Yes. He was in our bedroom, at the armoire, and he was shoving all our photographs into a bag. He even took our wedding picture."

"And then he hit you?" B.J. said.

"After he hung up the phone and I confronted him, yes."

"Who was he talking to?" Mick asked. "Do you know?"

"I . . ." Mrs. Charbonneau ran a hand through her hair. "He was talking to a woman, I think, and said he'd pick her up at her mother's in two hours."

"Her mother's," Mick repeated.

"Yes. Then he saw me. I demanded he tell me where ChiChi was, but he didn't say a word. He just pushed past me, shoved me actually, and I fell. I don't remember anything else."

"But why would he want their pictures?" B.J. asked.

"Who knows," Mick said. "Jason and Carl always did do strange things. Maybe he forgot that Interpol had his picture anyway, or maybe he didn't know, and figured if he took all these we wouldn't have one to go by if we tried to go after him."

"He took all my pictures of ChiChi too," Mrs. Charbonneau said.

As the paramedics arrived and began looking after Lillian, Mick urged B.J. toward the car. Once on their way back to the city, he flipped open his phone and dialed NOPD. "Jarrett, you got an address on Evie Strindel's mother?"

Fifteen minutes later they were in front of a large, century-old house just off Magazine.

"Must have been nice once," Mick said, looking at the dilapidated old building as they walked toward it.

B.J. knocked on the door.

"It's empty." Mick bent to peer into a window, then walked around to the back. He stopped beside a garbage can. "Someone had a dog, but the last time he was fed here, I'd say, was quite a few days ago."

"So do your thing, James Bond," B.J. said, moving to stand beside him, "and get us inside."

Mick's brows soared in mock surprise. "Aren't you the one who was worried that was illegal?"

"I'm not the one doing the breaking and entering," B.J. said.

He laughed. "No, just the entering."

"Whatever." She shoved him toward the building's back door.

"Well, whoever lives here lives sparse," B.J. said, walking into the living room. She saw an answering machine on an end table, but its message light was off. "So much for that," she said to herself. Picking up the phone, she pressed the redial button.

"Good afternoon, Hotel Meauthiere. How may I direct your call?"

B.J. pulled the receiver away from her ear, then hung up. She turned to Mick. "He didn't say 'mother's,'" she said excitedly, "he said 'Meauthiere's.'"

"Huh?"

"It's a small hotel in the Quarter. Meauthiere's."

THIRTEEN

The clerk looked at Mick's badge. "What can I do for you, Marshal?" she asked, purring slightly in spite of her obvious effort to remain businesslike.

B.J. nearly groaned. Did every woman in America swoon over Mick Gentry?

A little voice in the back of her mind answered: *No, you're just jealous.*

No, I'm not, she silently argued.

Yes, you are.

Mick showed the clerk the picture of Theodore Charbonneau from Lillian's studio. "Is this man registered here?"

"His name?" the clerk said.

"He'd be using an alias. Do you recognize him?"

She waved at another clerk. "I just came back from vacation, sorry." She took the photo and showed it to the other clerk as he approached. "Larry, do you know if this man is registered here?"

Larry dug a pair of glasses from his pocket and looked at the photo, then at Mick. "Yeah, that's Mr. Landers. He's here with his wife, but they're not in right now. I saw them leave a couple of hours ago."

Mick cursed softly and snatched the picture from Larry's hand.

"Have they had a dog with them?" B.J. asked. "A poodle."

Larry nodded. "Yeah, but the dog hasn't been around the last couple of days. Mrs. Landers said they couldn't take it with them." He shrugged. "I guess she meant when they leave here."

Mick pocketed the photo. "Don't mention to them that we've been here."

Both clerks nodded.

"I have an idea," B.J. said, walking toward the entry door.

"That sounds like trouble."

She turned to glare at Mick, but he was smiling. After weaving their way down three blocks crowded with costumed revelers, B.J. directed him into a boutique. She waved at the woman behind the counter. "Mary, hi. We're on a case and need to hide. Got anything left?"

The woman smiled. "In the back. Should be a few things left back there."

B.J. steered Mick toward the back of the store. "If we're going to stake out the hotel and not be seen, we need costumes."

"Costumes?" Mick moaned. "I haven't worn a costume since I was a kid at Halloween."

"Then pretend," B.J. said, "that it's Halloween."

Mick sneered. "Thanks."

"You're welcome. Here's one that's perfect for you." She handed him a gorilla suit.

"Fine," he said, grabbing the brown hairy outfit. "If this is perfect for me, then you wear this one." He handed her a witch's outfit.

"Oh, real nice, Marshal," B.J. said. "You really know how to flatter a girl."

"Flattery is as flattery does," he mocked.

"Oh, shut up." She pulled the black witch's dress over her own clothes and crunched the hat onto her head.

"Here's your nose," Mick said, handing her the rubber appendage that looked more like a finger, complete with black wart on its end.

"At least you can walk naturally now," B.J. countered, "and not feel out of place when your knuckles drag the ground."

Mick grabbed B.J.'s arm. "Just be careful out there," he said, his voice suddenly a little too deep, a little too emotional. "Don't take any foolish chances."

B.J. stared up at him. "You too," she said softly, suddenly wanting to fling her arms around him. She squeezed her fingers around her broom handle instead.

"I'll bet my last dollar that's Evie," B.J. said, nodding toward a blonde approaching the hotel.

"Stay here." Mick stepped off the curb and started to walk toward the woman.

As if having a sixth sense that he was a cop, in spite of the fact that he was dressed as a gorilla, Evie stopped and

Tricks of the Trade

looked straight at him, then spun and ran back down the banquette the way she'd come, shoving past people as she went.

At the same moment that Mick bolted after Evie, B.J. spotted a man dressed as King Arthur pause just a few yards to the left of the hotel's entrance. He watched Evie disappear into the crowd, then turned and hurried in the opposite direction.

"Theodore," B.J. said to herself, still unable to refer to him naturally as Jason Townsend. Dropping her broom, she dashed across the street and ran in the direction he had taken. Her head immediately began to throb. A wave of weakness washed over her, and she shrugged it away. Now was no time for that. She summoned every ounce of strength she had, knowing she couldn't let him get away. B.J. pushed through a throng of costumed revelers, turned the corner onto Canal, and was confronted by a virtual wall of people gathered to watch the grand parade of Comus.

"Great, just great," she muttered, as a man in a clown suit practically squashed her up against a brick wall in his efforts to pass. She began to push her way through the crowd in the direction Theodore had disappeared and was attacked by a cluster of feathers. Swatting at them and spitting one from her mouth, B.J. moved away from Mr. Peacock, or whatever the man thought he was dressed as, stood on her tiptoes, and searched for Theodore.

"Throw me one, mister," the young girl beside her suddenly yelled. She jumped up, knocking into B.J., to catch a plastic beaded necklace.

The thing caught on the point of B.J.'s black hat and slid down to settle on the crown. She looked at the man on the passing float who'd thrown it. He was dressed as King Arthur, as was every other man on the float, of which there had to be . . . she stopped counting at ten.

"What better place to hide than in plain sight," she mumbled. B.J. pushed past the people between her and the street, receiving a few curses and elbow jabs for her trouble. The float had stopped, and every King Arthur was busy throwing Mardi Gras beads and coins to the cheering crowd.

B.J. looked at each costumed king, about to decide her suspicion was ridiculous when she spotted her man at the rear of the float.

Someone shoved his way past B.J., knocking her into the side of the float. Her fake nose fell off and her King Arthur looked down.

B.J. jumped onto the float just as he started to dart to the other side. She reached out and caught his leg. Kicking her away, he twisted around, lost his balance, and fell into the crowd.

"You okay?" Mick yelled a second later.

She pushed herself out of the fake flowers she'd fallen into and looked up. Mick was standing beside the float, with Townsend—either Jason or Carl, she didn't know which—standing beside him, his right wrist handcuffed to Evie Strindel's left.

"I'm fine," she grumbled, not at all happy to have fallen face first onto the floor of a float while Mick captured not only his quarry, but hers too. Swinging her legs over the side of the float, she pushed off of it, but rather

Tricks of the Trade

than merely landing on the ground, she found herself securely wrapped within one of Mick's arms and crushed up against his chest.

"You're sure you're okay?" he asked, slightly breathless, his eyes as dark with emotion as his voice was deep.

Suddenly the fact that he had two people handcuffed to his other hand, that they were surrounded by hundreds of people, and that another float was slowly inching its way toward them, didn't matter. All she could think about was Mick, that he was safe and holding her in his arms.

His lips brushed lightly across hers. "That was a fool thing to do," he whispered huskily, "when you should really still be lying in bed."

Before she could respond he released her and turned to his prisoners, shoving them through the crowd and back toward the hotel entrance. "Guess who was trying to climb into a big, black car when I caught up with her?" Mick said over his shoulder.

B.J. stared at Evie. "*She* tried to run me down?"

"He told me to," Evie shrieked. "It was Carter's idea. He said you were getting too close."

B.J. frowned, until she remembered that Lola had said Evie's boyfriend was named Carter.

Once at the hotel Mick stopped and began searching Theodore's pockets. "Hey, what's this?" Mick said, holding up an envelope.

B.J. took it from him and looked inside. "Fake ID papers," she said. "For both of them."

"Yeah," Evie said, "and if they'd arrived on time, we would have been gone by now." She looked at Theodore, but it wasn't a look B.J. would term as loving. "Do you ever do anything right?" she said with a sneer.

"So, Jason," Mick said, smiling, "you are Jason, right?"

"He's Jason," Jarrett said, entering the interrogation room and tossing a folder onto the desk. "Prints confirm it."

"We know everything but why you killed Carl," Mick said. "Want to tell us?"

"I didn't kill Carl," Jason said.

B.J. sat in a corner, watching. He wasn't a handsome man, and obviously never had been, but at least in the picture Lillian Charbonneau had given her he'd looked somewhat debonair. Now his graying hair seemed thinner, his jowls fleshier, and his clothes were rumpled from being under the King Arthur costume.

"So who did?" Mick asked.

"It was an accident," he answered grudgingly.

Mick's brows rose. "An accident?" he echoed. "Carl comes looking for you to get his money and just conveniently ends up accidentally taking a bullet in his head."

"I tripped," Jason snapped. "Okay, I tripped. I was supposed to get Carl some fake ID papers so he could get out of the country, and he wanted fifty thousand dollars. I couldn't get that kind of money without Lillian finding out, and if she found out . . ." he sighed deeply, then slammed a hand onto the table. "If she'd have found out about my past, she would have divorced me and I'd have had nothing." He glanced from Mick to Jarrett. "Nothing, you understand? I wasn't going to go back to having nothing."

"So you killed Carl so you could hang on to your comfortable life with your wife," Jarrett said.

"No. Yes. I mean . . ." He sat forward, shaking his head and sending wisps of gray hair falling into his face. "It was an accident. I tried to tell Carl I couldn't get the money, not that much anyhow, and he blew up, started waving his gun around and saying if I didn't get the money he'd kill me, and maybe Evie, too, just for good measure."

Mick glanced at B.J., then at Jarrett.

Jason ran both hands back over his head. Fear shone in his eyes. "I was scared, dammit," he said. "For Evie. I grabbed the gun, just to get it away from him." He shrugged and sank back in his chair, the life suddenly seeming to flow out of him like air out of a balloon. "I don't know what happened. Carl kept yelling, I tried to yank the gun away from him, and it went off. The next thing I knew Evie was screaming, the damned dog was howling, and Carl was lying on the ground dead, his false teeth shattered and half sticking out of his mouth."

"That's why you tossed them?" Mick said.

He looked up, a scornful expression in his eyes. "No. Once I realized Carl was dead I figured I'd make it look like it was me, like I'd taken money out of Lillian's accounts, couldn't live with my guilt, and committed suicide. I took the teeth and tossed them later so you guys couldn't ID the body."

"That's why you started the fire," Jarrett said.

"Yeah. And I got Lillian's money out of the bank, and

fake ID papers, and tickets to Bermuda for me and Evie." He glanced at B.J. "Then she started nosing around after the damned dog."

She smiled. "So why didn't you just let me find the dog and be on your way?"

"Cause Evie fell in love with the mutt, that's why." He shook his head in disbelief. "I never could say no to Evie."

"What about the ring?" Jarrett asked.

Mick smiled and answered before Jason could. "Jason always liked flashy jewelry. That's why he got in trouble in Europe, right, Jason? Lifting some guy's Rolex?"

B.J. stood and walked to the table. "Where's ChiChi?"

"I don't know. Stupid dog. Didn't even know the mutt was in my car 'til I picked Evie up."

B.J. left the room while Jarrett and Mick continued to question Jason. She walked into an interrogation room farther down the hall. "Evie," she said, sitting down across the table from the woman. "I need to know where ChiChi is."

The stripper's eyes filled with tears. "You aren't going to take him to the pound or nothing, are you? 'Cause he's okay. I mean, where he's at. He's being taken care of."

B.J. shook her head. "No, I'm not taking him to the pound. Mrs. Charbonneau wants him back."

Evie nodded. "Yeah, I guess she's got a right." She sniffed. "He's with my mom, up at her sister's place in Metairie."

Mick stepped from interrogation room number One and into the hall at the same time that B.J. stepped from interrogation room Two. Their gazes met, and for the brief flash of a millisecond nothing else mattered.

Then Mick pulled back. It wasn't a physical thing, but B.J. knew it might as well have been, because she not only felt it but saw it. He closed down, right there in front of her, and the pain that lanced her heart was almost more than she could bear.

She forced a smile to her face. "Well, that about does it," she said brightly. She should have known better than to get involved with him. Hadn't she had enough experience with men to be able to spot the danger signs? A sneer tugged at one corner of her mouth. Obviously not, she told herself.

"I'll take you home," Mick said, then wished he hadn't. What he really wanted to do was pull her into his arms and hold her close, crush her against his body and never let go. He wanted to cover her mouth with his and taste the sweetness of her kiss until he was so intoxicated, his senses were reeling. He wanted to feel her naked body pressed to his and make love to her until he was too weak to move, too exhausted even to draw another breath. And he wanted to lose his soul within hers so he would never have to leave her, never have to be alone again.

He stiffened, drawing his shoulders back. Nice thoughts, he told himself, but totally unreasonable. A U.S. marshal and a P.I. wouldn't have made a very promising combination in normal circumstances. With Mick's history thrown into the equation, he figured the odds were about a zillion to one. He'd already tried to combine marriage, family, and his job, and it had proven a disaster. He didn't need to try it again, or hurt her any more than he already had.

"I can get a cab," B.J. said. There was no use prolonging this thing. She shouldn't have let him into her life. Now he wanted out. Bon soir, sayonara, arrivederci, Roma, and all that stuff.

"I'll take you home," Mick said again, a little more sternly than he'd meant to. He didn't know why he was insisting on it; he just knew that he didn't want to say good-bye to her yet.

They walked to his car in silence.

"Dumb," B.J. muttered. "Dumb, dumb, dumb." But calling herself names didn't make her feel any better, and neither did continually thinking about Mick Gentry. She pushed thoughts of him from her mind and looked at the check lying on the seat next to her purse. True to her word, Mrs. Charbonneau had paid a bundle to get her precious little ChiChi back, and now B.J. had enough money to relax. She could pay her bills, buy a few new suits, put a little in the bank, and still have plenty of working capital left for the agency.

Beaujolais scrambled over the seat and plopped down next to her bag.

"Well, I guess you're not mad at me anymore for bringing another dog into the car and making you ride in the back seat."

Beaujolais barked, then turned several circles on the seat and lay down.

She dug a treat out of her purse and held it out to him.

Beaujolais took it daintily, swallowed instantly, and licked B.J.'s hand.

"Well, I had decided I hated all men," she said, rubbing his head, "but I guess I'll make an exception for you."

Mick looked at the empty suitcase on his bed, then turned and walked to the window. He had a plane to catch in the morning and should be packing, but he couldn't seem to bring himself to do it. Instead he stared out at the streets of the Quarter. A sliver of a moon hung in the dark sky, streetlights cast a soft glow over the walls of the ancient buildings, a few stalwart tourists still wandered the sidewalks here and there, and an old horse-drawn carriage moved past the hotel just as a small sports car pulled up to the entrance. Mick saw it all without really seeing it because his mind was filled with images and thoughts of B.J. He wanted to be with her more than he had wanted anything in a very long time. Yet he knew that a relationship between himself and B.J. couldn't work.

A knock on the door startled him. Mick glanced at the watch on his wrist. It was late, and he hadn't ordered any room service. Crossing the room, he opened the door. "B.J.," Mick said, staring at her.

She held his dark glasses out to him. "These must have fallen out of your jacket pocket when you were at my place."

Mick stared at the aviator-style glasses, not wanting to

take them for fear his fingers might brush against hers. If he touched her, he knew he'd be lost, unable to stop himself from pulling her into his arms.

B.J. looked past him. "Packing?" she said, seeing the suitcase lying open on the bed.

He shrugged, trying to seem nonchalant and wishing the knot in his throat would go away. "The case is wrapped up," he said, his voice harsh with suppressed emotion. "But they'll have another waiting for me."

She wanted to yell at him, to damn him for making her fall in love with him only so she'd have to watch him walk out of her life. B.J. swallowed hard. Love. She hadn't actually used that word before in reference to her feelings for him. She was in love with him, and he was going to leave her. But not yet, she told herself. She couldn't let him go yet. "Well, since you're going to be leaving," she tried to sound light, "why don't we have a late dinner together? Kind of a good-bye thing. Unless you've already eaten?"

Mick was about to say no, he was tired, had to get up early, maybe he'd call her sometime, which was a lie, when he saw the yearning passion in her eyes, heard the catch in her voice, felt the tremor that ran through her fingers as she reached out and touched his arm ever so lightly. He knew then that he had to tell her the truth so she'd understand why her yearnings were wasted on him, why he knew she could do better than to love Mick Gentry. He owed her that much.

"Let's go for a walk," he said, grabbing his jacket from a nearby chair. "There's something I need to tell you." He paused while shutting the door behind him and looked deep into her eyes, knowing it might be the last time he'd see warmth and desire for him there. He was about to destroy that, and the thought nearly sliced him in two. "Then if you still want to go to dinner, we'll go."

But he knew she wouldn't.

FOURTEEN

With a hand only barely touching the curve of her back, Mick guided B.J. onto the path that wound its way through Jackson Square. "Four years ago I had a wife and son," Mick said.

B.J. kept her gaze on the large statue of Andrew Jackson they were approaching, its aged bronze lines softly reflecting the muted light of the square's lamps, while its inward curves remained steeped in shadow. Her arms were crossed beneath her breasts and now she was glad, because the pose hid the small start of surprise when she heard his words—not that he'd had a wife, but that he'd had a son.

"We were at the home of my partner, having dinner." The pain of dredging up all the old memories, especially of Kyle and what had happened, cut into Mick as deeply as if it had all happened only hours before, but he knew it had to be done: He had to do this for B.J.

She glanced at him furtively as they continued to

walk, saw the hurt that came into his eyes, heard it in his voice, and wanted to reach out to him, but restrained herself, instinctively knowing that it would be the wrong thing to do.

"Kyle was playing cops and robbers with Jack's son Robby," Mick continued, "both of them running around the house, in one room, out another, while Jack and I cooked steaks out on the patio barbecue and our wives fixed the other stuff in the kitchen."

He fell silent for a moment, alone with his memories.

B.J. thought she knew what was coming and prayed she was wrong.

"Jack was usually very careful with his gun, but we'd been out late the night before, he was exhausted, and . . ." Mick inhaled deeply. "We didn't know the boys had gotten hold of Jack's gun until it was too late."

She felt her breath catch in her throat, her heart threaten to stop its incessantly steady beat. *No*, something deep down inside of her cried. *Not that.*

"Kyle died instantly," Mick said, dashing any hope she had that she was wrong.

B.J. felt the pain that swept over him at voicing the horror of his memory, as much as if it had been her own. Then she realized that his pain was her pain, because she loved him.

Mick forced himself to go on and ignore the tears that stung the back of his eyes at the memory of the day his son had been ripped away from him. "Five months later Sherry left. Our marriage had been in trouble before Kyle's death—at least Sherry said it had, I just hadn't been around enough to notice."

He paused beneath the moss-laden limb of an old oak tree and turned to look at B.J. "She said I'd been too preoccupied with my job to be a good husband and father."

"It takes two to make a marriage work," B.J. said, not knowing what else to say.

Mick shook his head. "Yeah, but in my case there was only one working at saving the marriage, and it wasn't me." He looked deep into B.J.'s eyes. "Sherry was right. I wasn't there. I didn't realize it at the time, but I wasn't there for my family. My job took me away from them, mentally and physically, and I let it." Against his will, he reached out and touched her cheek lightly with his fingertips. "I can't change, B.J., and I can't cause you that same kind of pain. You need a man who can offer you everything, who can be there for you when you need him, when your kids need him. You deserve that. You deserve a regular, normal life, and as much as I want to, I know I can't provide one."

His hand dropped away from her, and B.J. felt emptier for the loss of his touch. She wanted to cry, but she wasn't going to. And she wasn't going to lose Mick Gentry either, if she could help it. B.J. moved closer to him, placing her hands on his chest. His warm breath stirred the hair at her temple and caressed the curve of her cheek. She sensed the resistance in him, heard the catch of his breath at her nearness, and felt him start at her touch and steel himself against it.

"I would never want you to change," she said softly. "But don't lie to me, or to yourself."

His eyes narrowed and his shoulders drew back. "B.J.,

Tricks of the Trade

don't," he said, his voice hoarse with emotion. He ached to reach out to her, to wrap her in his arms, and struggled to resist the urge.

"You need love as badly as I do, Mick Gentry," B.J. said, "and you have a lot of it to offer, if you'd just let yourself."

He shook his head. "I told you—"

"You told me excuses," she said, cutting him off. She took a deep breath and plunged ahead, knowing this was it, all or nothing, and she had no intention of accepting nothing gracefully. She loved Mick Gentry and wanted him in her life more than anything she'd ever wanted. The mere thought of losing him fired a determination within her that gave her the strength and courage she needed to continue. "We're two of a kind, Mick. Strong, independent, bull-headed, and stubborn. If we're going to make it through this life at all, we'd probably be much better off doing it together than struggling through it apart." She fought the tears that filled her eyes, but it was a losing battle. "Don't deny us this chance, Mick," B.J. whispered. "Don't deny us this love."

He watched as her tears hovered on her lashes for a split second, then fell silently onto her cheeks and ran downward in a river of silver, and the last few barricades still standing around his heart crumbled and fell away.

For the past four years something had been missing from his life. He'd tried to ignore it, to deny that he needed to love someone, and that he needed someone to love him. Pulling her into his arms, Mick's lips crushed down upon hers and the last shreds of his loneliness were swept away. "I do love you, B.J." He laughed softly, his lips against her hair as he held her tightly. "I love you so much, I think I must have been crazy to think I could live without you."

More tears flowed from B.J.'s eyes, but this time they weren't tears of sadness. She pulled away from him slightly to look into his eyes. "We'll work it out," she said.

He smiled, and it was like sunshine pouring into her heart. "I know we will," Mick said, "but it will be easier than you think."

B.J. frowned. "What do you mean?"

"I mean," he said, his hands sliding down her back to her waist and holding her cradled in his embrace, "I'm going to ask for a transfer and make New Orleans my homebase. I want you to be my wife and the mother of my children."

Her heart suddenly seemed so full, she didn't think she could handle it anymore. She'd been afraid, because of what had happened to his son, that even if he did stay with her, he would never want another child. "Are you sure, Mick?" she whispered, still half afraid he would say no.

He brushed his lips lightly across hers, then stared down into her eyes, blue melding with blue, and he silently promised her a lifetime of tomorrows, an eternity of sunshine. "I've never been more sure of anything in my life. But I believe that, once we have the pitter-patter of little feet running through out house, one or the other of us should be home for them at all times, so we'll just have to work out our schedules so that we're not both chasing down crooks at the same time." One golden brow rose slightly as he looked down at her. "Deal?"

B.J. smiled, convinced she was the happiest woman in the world. "You've got yourself a deal, Marshal," she said, slipping her arms around his neck. "I just hope you're prepared for it, because I'm never going to let you get out of it."

"The thought never crossed my mind," Mick whispered as his lips covered hers.

THE EDITORS' CORNER

Happy anniversary! No, not you—us! June 1997 marks the fourteenth anniversary of LOVESWEPT. Many of you have been with us since the inception of LOVESWEPT. For that, we thank you and we hope to continue our strong relationship with our loyal readers. Speaking of relationships, have we got some doozies for you! Our fourteenth anniversary lineup includes everything from corporate intrigue, pretend weddings, diamonds, and babies. (And not necessarily in that order!) Oh yeah, remember last month's editors' corner where we told you to keep an eye out for that "new, yet traditional look" in LOVESWEPT's future? Well, the future is now, baby!

With his company at stake as well as his heart, Rio Thornton must guard himself from the golden-eyed corporate princess Yasmine Damaron in **THE DAMARON MARK: THE HEIRESS,** LOVE-

SWEPT #838, by bestselling author Fayrene Preston. A trademark Damaron, Yasmine is very much in control of herself and her heart, but when she faces the fiercely masculine executive, the heat of his desire stuns and arouses her. She makes Rio an offer he can't refuse, insisting that she's only after his business, but Rio's heart is the soul of his business. Can he give his heart away without losing the one thing he needs most? With a story that's both sensual and charming, Fayrene Preston is back, in this latest installment of the Damaron series.

In Destiny, Texas, there is a force at work: a fortune-teller with mystical powers of foresight. However, in Karen Leabo's **BRIDES OF DESTINY: MILLICENT'S MEDICINE MAN**, LOVESWEPT #839, Millicent Whitney, a widow and expectant mother, refuses to believe that Dr. Jase Desmond is the one for her. She's already had the love of her life and now he's dead, leaving her with a baby on the way. Way out of his league, neurosurgeon Jase Desmond helps to deliver Millicent's baby and realizes that he's been denying himself for far too long. Can Jase teach Millicent that loving again isn't betraying a memory but opening her heart to new dreams? In this poignant love story of new beginnings and second chances, Karen Leabo explores the funny and tender side of starting over, with this last chapter of the Brides of Destiny series.

Suzanne Brockmann returns with another sexy and charming comedy in **STAND-IN GROOM**, LOVESWEPT #840. Chelsea Spencer has to get married in order to receive her inheritance, but the man she's chosen has just RSVPed his regrets. Suddenly she remembers the handsome (and interested) stranger who'd saved her from being mugged. When she offers Johnny Anziano the opportunity to make his dreams come true, Johnny jumps at the chance to get to know Chelsea, even if it includes marrying her first. Chelsea and Johnny's shaky alliance means a risky marital charade and a spirited romp that is irresistibly seductive and utterly romantic.

Fate. Faith. The laws of divine reciprocity. Drake Tallen has his own word to define the priceless gem he found: Justice. In **FLAWLESS**, LOVESWEPT #841, Drake knows that this perfect gem will lure Emery Brooks back home long enough for him to exact his sweet revenge on his almost-bride-to-be. Ten years ago, Emery had run from the small Indiana town to an empty life in Chicago. Now tasked with buying the gem from Drake, Emery must face the man she loved and left, but can she resist his dark desire and the memories too strong to deny? And can she do it without surrendering her heart for the perfect stone? Cynthia Powell's latest novel delivers one surprise after another in a story sizzling with sensual secrets.

Happy reading!

With warmest wishes,

Shauna Summers

Joy Abella

Shauna Summers
Editor

Joy Abella
Administrative Editor

P.S. Look for these Bantam women's fiction titles coming in June. *New York Times* bestselling author Amanda Quick stuns the romance world with **AFFAIR**. Private investigator Charlotte Arkendale doesn't know what to make of Baxter St. Ives, her new man-of-affairs. He claims to be a respectable gentleman, but something in his eyes proclaims otherwise. Fellow *New York Times* bestselling author Nora Roberts delivers **SWEET REVENGE**, now available again in paperback. Just as Princess Adrianne is poised to taste the sweetness of her long-awaited vengeance, she finds herself up against two formidable men—one with the knowledge to take her freedom, the other with the power to take her life. In the tradition of PRINCE OF SHADOWS and PRINCE OF WOLVES, Susan Krinard returns with **TWICE A HERO**. Adventurer Mac Sinclair is fascinated by the exploits of her grandfather and his partner Liam O'Shea. When she becomes disoriented inside the ruins in the Mayan jungles, she bumps into Liam O'Shea himself . . . alive, well, and seductively real—in the year 1884! Historical romance favorite Adrienne deWolfe puts the finishing touch on her Texas trilogy with **TEXAS WILDCAT**, a story about a man and a woman who are on opposite sides of the fence. As Bailey McShane and Zach Rawlins struggle with the drought that's tearing the state apart, they slowly realize that being together is the thing that matters most.

Don't miss these extraordinary books
by your favorite Bantam authors!

On sale in April:

MISCHIEF
by *Amanda Quick*

ONCE A WARRIOR
by *Karyn Monk*

Now available in paperback

MISCHIEF

by *New York Times* bestselling author

Amanda Quick

To help her foil a ruthless fortune hunter, Imogen Waterstone needs a man.
Not just any man, but Matthias Marshall, the intrepid explorer known as
"Cold-blooded Colchester."

"You pass yourself off as a man of action, but now it seems that you are not that sort of man at all," Imogen told Matthias.

"I do not pass myself off as anything but what I am, you exasperating little—"

"Apparently you write fiction rather than fact, sir. Bad enough that I thought you to be a clever, resourceful gentleman given to feats of daring. I have also been laboring under the equally mistaken assumption that you are a man who would put matters of honor ahead of petty considerations of inconvenience."

"Are you calling my honor as well as my manhood into question?"

"Why shouldn't I? You are clearly indebted to

me, sir, yet you obviously wish to avoid making payment on that debt."

"I was indebted to your uncle, not to you."

"I have explained to you that I inherited the debt," she retorted.

Matthias took another gliding step into the grim chamber. "Miss Waterstone, you try my patience."

"I would not dream of doing so," she said, her voice dangerously sweet. "I have concluded that you will not do at all as an associate in my scheme. I hereby release you from your promise. Begone, sir."

"Bloody hell, woman. You are not going to get rid of me so easily." Matthias crossed the remaining distance between them with two long strides and clamped his hands around her shoulders.

Touching her was a mistake. Anger metamorphosed into desire in the wink of an eye.

For an instant he could not move. His insides seemed to have been seized by a powerful fist. Matthias tried to breathe, but Imogen's scent filled his head, clouding his brain. He looked down into the bottomless depths of her blue-green eyes and wondered if he would drown. He opened his mouth to conclude the argument with a suitably repressive remark, but the words died in his throat.

The outrage vanished from Imogen's gaze. It was replaced by sudden concern. "My lord? Is something wrong?"

"Yes." It was all he could do to get the word past his teeth.

"What is it?" She began to look alarmed. "Are you ill?"

"Quite possibly."

"Good heavens. I had not realized. That no doubt explains your odd behavior."

"No doubt."

"Would you care to lie down on the bed for a few minutes?"

"I do not think that would be a wise move at this juncture." She was so soft. He could feel the warmth of her skin through the sleeves of her prim, practical gown. He realized that he longed to discover if she made love with the same impassioned spirit she displayed in an argument. He forced himself to remove his hands from her shoulders. "We had best finish this discussion at some other time."

"Nonsense," she said bracingly. "I do not believe in putting matters off, my lord."

Matthias shut his eyes for the space of two or three seconds and took a deep breath. When he lifted his lashes he saw that Imogen was watching him with a fascinated expression. "Miss Waterstone," he began with grim determination. "I am trying to employ reason here."

"You're going to help me, aren't you?" She started to smile.

"I beg your pardon?"

"You've changed your mind, haven't you? Your sense of honor has won out." Her eyes glowed. "Thank you, my lord. I knew you would assist me in my plans." She gave him an approving little pat on the arm. "And you must not concern yourself with the other matter."

"What other matter?"

"Why, your lack of direct experience with bold feats and daring adventure. I quite understand. You need not be embarrassed by the fact that you are not a man of action, sir."

"Miss Waterstone—"

"Not everyone can be an intrepid sort, after all," she continued blithely. "You need have no fear. If anything dangerous occurs in the course of my scheme, I shall deal with it."

"The very thought of you taking charge of a dangerous situation is enough to freeze the marrow in my bones."

"Obviously you suffer from a certain weakness of the nerves. But we shall contrive to muddle through. Try not to succumb to the terrors of the imagination, my lord. I know you must be extremely anxious about what lies ahead, but I assure you, I will be at your side every step of the way."

"Will you, indeed?" He felt dazed.

"I shall protect you." Without any warning, Imogen put her arms around him and gave him what was no doubt meant to be a quick, reassuring hug.

The tattered leash Matthias was using to hold on to his self-control snapped. Before Imogen could pull away, he wrapped her close.

"Sir?" Her eyes widened with surprise.

"The only aspect of this situation that truly alarms me, Miss Waterstone," he said roughly, "is the question of who will protect me from you?"

Her stories are tender and sensual, humorous and deeply involving. Now Karyn Monk offers her most enthralling romance ever . . . a tale of a shattered hero fighting for redemption—and fighting for love. . . .

ONCE A WARRIOR

Karyn Monk

"Karyn Monk . . . brings the romance of the era to readers with her spellbinding storytelling talents. This is a new author to watch."
—*Romantic Times*

Ariella MacKendrick knew her people had only one hope for survival: she must find the mighty warrior known as the Black Wolf and bring him home to defend her clan. But when Ariella finally tracks him down, Malcolm MacFane is nothing like the hero she dreamed he would be. The fearless laird who once led a thousand men is a drunken shell of his former self, scarred inside and out, with no army in sight. Yet Ariella has no choice but to put her trust in MacFane.

And soon something begins to stir in the fallen legend. A fire still rages in his warrior heart—a passion that could lead them into battle . . . a desire, barely leashed, that could brand a Highland beauty's soul.

"Turn onto your stomach, MacFane," she instructed quietly.

He did not argue but simply did as she told him. Ariella suspected the powder she had given him had taken effect.

Now that he was on his front, it was far easier for her to massage him. She focused on the valley of his back for a while, and when she was finished, she placed one of the warm swine bladders on it, so the muscles could absorb the heat. Then she moved up, gently kneading the solid layers of spasm on each side of his spine. Little by little the hardness beneath her fingers began to yield. Her touch grew firmer, delved deeper, encouraging the muscles to release their grip. When her hands began to ache, she retrieved the other swine bladder, which she had kept warm before the fire, and gently placed it on his upper back.

MacFane's eyes were closed and he was breathing deeply, his head resting against his arm. Wanting him to be as comfortable as possible, Ariella removed his boots, examining his injured leg as she did so. He had told her it was shattered when his horse collapsed on it. She ran her hands up the muscled calf, bent it slightly at the knee, then continued her journey along his thigh. The bone seemed straight enough, and from what she could tell he had not lost any length. But she knew a bad break could plague a person with pain for the rest of his life. The leg was stiff, so she rubbed some ointment into her palms and began to massage it. After watching him limp this past month, she wondered if there was anything that could be done to ease the ache and strengthen the muscles. Perhaps with exercise—

"I didn't fall."

She looked up at him, surprised that he was still awake. "Pardon?"

"I didn't fall," he repeated thickly. "Someone put a spur under my saddle."

"I know." She continued to massage his leg.

He nodded with satisfaction and closed his eyes again. "I'm not in the habit of falling off my goddamn horse." The words were slurred, but she could hear the anger in them.

She thought of him thundering into her camp wielding his sword in both hands. No, MacFane was not in the habit of falling off his horse. Someone was trying to drive him away. The arrow hadn't worked, so they put a spur under his saddle, knowing the fall would not only injure him physically but would humiliate him in front of the entire clan.

"I think it was Niall," he mumbled.

She paused. "Why do you say that?"

"He has never tried to hide his contempt for me." He lifted his lids and regarded her a moment, his blue eyes suddenly intense. "And I've seen the way he looks at you." His expression was dark, as if the matter angered him. Then he sighed and closed his eyes once more.

Ariella considered this. Niall had shared her loathing toward MacFane when he failed to answer her father's missive. She had even encouraged his fury when her clan was attacked and MacFane never came. But while she could understand his expressing his contempt, could Niall actually be trying to drive him away? To do so would not be in the best interest of the clan. Was it possible his rage was that great?

Deeply disturbed by the possibility, she removed the cooling swine bladders from MacFane's back. He shifted onto his side, his head still resting on the hard pillow of his arm, his dark brown hair spilling loosely over his massive shoulder. Deciding she would bind his ribs with the linen strips tomorrow, she drew a blanket over him, then stayed there a moment, studying him.

He exuded an extraordinary aura of power and vulnerability as he lay there, injured and drugged, yet somehow still formidable. How cruelly ironic, that after fighting so many battles as the great Black Wolf, his greatest enemy now was his own body. Perhaps she had asked too much of him by bringing him here to train her people. From early morning to late evening he labored, training, planning, overseeing the fortifications to the castle. His demanding days would exhaust a man at the peak of his physical abilities, never mind one for whom it was an effort to cross a room or mount the stairs. And now someone was determined to force him from here, even if it meant injuring him in the process. It was wrong to expect he should remain under such circumstances, even if he had promised to remain until they found a new laird. She must send him away as soon as he was fit to ride, before he was even more injured than he had been today. In his current state he could do nothing more to help them. It was now up to her to find a warrior with an army who could wield the sword.

Yet as she stood beside him watching the even rise and fall of his chest, she could not help but wonder what would happen to MacFane when he left. He had no family or clan who would joyously celebrate his return. Instead he would go back to the dank, filthy hut he shared with Gavin, where his days would be nothing but long, empty hours filled with pain, drink, and bitterness. While this fact had never bothered her before, suddenly she found the idea abhorrent. However MacFane had failed his people, did he really deserve to be condemned to such a miserable existence?

His brow was creased, indicating he still struggled with his pain. He moaned slightly and buried his face in his arm, as if trying to escape his discomfort. A dark lock of hair slipped across the clenched line of his jaw. Without thinking, Ariella leaned over and gently brushed the hair off his face, her fingers grazing the sandy surface of his cheek. MacFane's hand instantly clamped around her wrist, binding her to him with bruising force.

He opened his eyes and glared at her, his gaze menacing as he fought to clear the mists of alcohol and herbs. When he realized who she was, his grip eased, but he did not release her. Instead he pulled her down, until she hovered barely a breath away from him.

"I will not leave you, Ariella," he whispered roughly, "until I know you are safe."

Ariella stared at him, her heart beating rapidly, wondering how he could have known what she was thinking. "You cannot stay, MacFane," she countered. "Whoever wants you gone will not stop until you are dead."

Malcolm released her wrist and waited for her to move away from him. When she did not, he hesitantly laid his fingers against her cheek. "I'm already dead," he murmured, fascinated by the softness of her skin. "I have been for a long time."

They stayed like that a moment, staring at each other. And then, overcome with weariness, Malcolm sighed and drifted into sleep, his hand still pressed against the silk of Ariella's cheek.

On sale in May:

AFFAIR
by *Amanda Quick*

TWICE A HERO
by *Susan Krinard*

TEXAS WILDCAT
by *Adrienne deWolfe*

DON'T MISS THESE FABULOUS BANTAM WOMEN'S FICTION TITLES

On Sale in April

from New York Times *bestseller*
AMANDA QUICK
comes

MISCHIEF

now available in paperback

____ 57190-7 $6.50/$8.99

from KARYN MONK

author of The Rebel and the Redcoat

ONCE A WARRIOR

A medieval Scottish tale of a Highland beauty desperate to save her clan, and a shattered hero fighting for redemption —and fighting for love.   ____ 57422-1 $5.99/$7.99

Ask for these books at your local bookstore or use this page to order.

Please send me the books I have checked above. I am enclosing $____ (add $2.50 to cover postage and handling). Send check or money order, no cash or C.O.D.'s, please.

Name _____

Address _____

City/State/Zip _____

Send order to: Bantam Books, Dept. FN158, 2451 S. Wolf Rd., Des Plaines, IL 60018
Allow four to six weeks for delivery.
Prices and availability subject to change without notice.   FN 158 4/97